A FATHER'S LOVE

By the same author:

J. J. Stories, Book Guild Publishing, 2005

A FATHER'S LOVE

Wendy Sadler

Book Guild Publishing
Sussex, England

First published in Great Britain in 2005 by
The Book Guild Ltd,
25 High Street,
Lewes, East Sussex
BN7 2LU

Typesetting in Baskerville by
IML Typographers, Birkenhead, Merseyside

Printed in Great Britain by
CPI Bath

A catalogue record for this book is available from
The British Library.

ISBN 1 85776 943 0

I would like to dedicate this book to my father, who always believed in me. I miss you, Dad

1

'Dead!' It was amazing the impact one word could have on your world. The one word that dredged up images of old people, succumbing at the end their fruitful lives to some disease or other, or just simply fading away. It did not apply to the young and it most definitely did not apply to his daughter! Not to his little Anne. *No – No – No. Please God, don't let it be true!*

But here he sat with the phone held tightly in his cold steel fingers. It was no longer attached to his ear. After the initial conversation, he had dropped his arm and the phone with it, hunching himself in the old chair that stood soullessly against the wall. He could vaguely hear the voice rambling on at the other end of the phone, but he didn't care any more. The worst had happened to him. There was nothing more in this world that could be taken from him. Nothing.

His wife had died five years before, but that death had been a merciful release from the cancer that had forced her to be bedridden for a year. Yes, it had been a relief to finally bury her, knowing her pain and suffering were over. And Anne had been there through it all, supporting him and helping him sort out her mother's clothes.

There had been a distinct distance between the two of them before the cancer was diagnosed. And then, of course, when the disease had really taken hold, how could he have left her? He simply couldn't and he had remained to nurse her, night after night. When the end came, it had been such a release. For both of them.

But Anne had been there, helping him. His beloved Anne. And now, some strange voice on the phone was telling him that she was dead. Not only was she dead, but she had been shot far away in Africa, where she had gone to work for the Red Cross.

He had worshipped her, his only child, from the moment he laid eyes on her in the hospital in Dublin. Her dark hair and deep violet eyes had twinkled up to him and he had fallen madly, deeply and unconditionally in love with her. And from that day on, they were seldom separated. It was only after the death of her mother that Anne had decided she would like to join the Red Cross, and he had reluctantly agreed. Oh God! How he wished he had stopped her.

His lean, frozen fingers let the phone drop and it banged noisily against the wall. Fragments of conversation swirled around him. '... can you identify the body ... Donnas ... we will fly you out ... so sorry ... is there anyone who we can call for you?...' But there was no one. He was now completely and utterly alone. A tall, frail, elderly man with stooping shoulders and nothing left to live for.

He leant his grey head against the white-washed wall and slowly his eyes hardened. He would go and identify her body and then he would make them pay. Hunching his shoulders, he buried his face in his hands and cried bitter tears. In the end there were no more tears to shed.

Weeks went by and then months. He stopped talking to his neighbours, and buried himself in his grief. And finally, half demented, he began to formulate his plan. They were going to pay for what they did. Whoever had stolen his beloved Anne was going to pay, and they were going to pay in blood. He was going to hunt them down. He didn't care if he died in the process as he didn't have anything to live for now. Not any more.

2

The bitter cold worked its way silently around the emotionally tortured young woman, who tried desperately to wrap the threadbare blanket further around her flimsy body. She shivered and looked up into the night sky, almost begging for a reprieve. In the distance, the light of a car reflected on the snow that surrounded her. She prayed it would stop. It didn't. But then, had she really expected it to? No, because no one knew she was there, or even cared. She was alone – totally alone. And she was afraid; afraid she would die right here in the bitter cold, surrounded by a blanket of soft white snow. So beautiful and yet so deadly. Even the orphanage where she had grown up and escaped from didn't seem so bad as this predicament she had got herself into.

The cold stone walls of the orphanage and the harsh matron felt like heaven at this moment. How she had got herself here she still wasn't too sure. But she had thought that Patrick would help her. He had rescued her once before from the matron so why would he not come when she had called him? She couldn't go home as she was certain that she would be killed, and opted instead to hide out. She knew the secret that that awful man was trying to keep and she had copied the sheet of paper with the information on.

At first she had been shocked at what was going on. But she had promised Patrick that she would get a temporary job at the British Embassy and see if she could find anything to help him. And she had found it, and now it lay burning a hole deep inside her pocket and Patrick was nowhere to help her. She was being hunted down like a criminal by people determined to prevent her from sharing her knowledge.

The cold, stark, steel bridge stood out against the Moscow sky, with the coloured lights of the city in the background. Snow covered the harsh ugliness of the bridge and the smell of death. Trees stood deathly quiet nearby and no birds dared to breathe. Everything seemed silent. Even the river lay frozen, reflecting a bare minimum of light off its icy surface. Dark figures danced briefly across the frozen surface as the moon bounced from one cloud to another. Beneath the ice surface lay the dark green murky water, moving slowly and sluggishly; just waiting for spring to arrive so that it could dump the rotting corpses that had frozen in its depths onto its banks. The river was ugly and sadistic in nature.

She was hidden from view and no one cared that she was alone and penniless – not really. She was just one of hundreds in an icy and heartless city. Moscow didn't tolerate weakness. Didn't tolerate her weaknesses, her moods, her life. It could have been so different. So wonderfully different. But sometimes, just sometimes, life makes your choices and you have no control over them. You have no choice! None. And that feels like a bottomless pit of despair. Nowhere to turn. Nowhere to run. All your life choices are robbed from you, leaving you with nothing. Absolutely nothing. And no one to comfort you, to say, 'It'll be all right in the morning.' Where was he? Why did he have to let her down this time, when she desperately needed him? Waiting here was perhaps the last chance she had. She had returned to the rendezvous frequently during the last few days, but this time was different. This time she felt as if the fight was slowly ebbing out of her. Why couldn't he just be here?

An anguished sigh escaped her blue-tinged lips, and the

warm moisture turned itself into tiny ice daggers just waiting to take their final stab at her emaciated, fragile body. Thankfully her face was too frozen to feel their gleefully inflicted pain. And she was almost too far along to care. Almost. Trying to curl up further, she hugged herself to retain body heat. It was useless. Her thin legs trembled from the cold, barely covered by her dark jeans. She looked at her bleak, stark surroundings. The ugliness seemed to congratulate her mood. Nothing in her situation or surroundings comforted her. She lay huddled in a heap of dirty snow just beneath the bridge. Somewhere in the distance she could hear a tiny trickle of water. Every now and then a small bundle of snow would plummet from the top of the bridge onto the icy surface of the water, scattering as far as it could.

The cold penetrated to the very core of her bones. Her eyelids grew heavy and she knew that it wouldn't be long before eternal sleep took over, and eternal peace would be her only concern.

Her mind began to play tricks on her. For a minute she dreamed that Patrick was running towards her with his arms open wide. Patrick, who had saved her from the orphanage. Patrick, her knight in shining armour. Patrick, who would save her from this disaster. It should never have got this far and it should not be allowed to take her life. Flinging her blanket back, she ran towards him and into his arms. And his warmth surrounded her icy heart. But, as her eyelids struggled open, she realised that the warm flower-filled fields were just the deep piles of cruel, merciless snow and ice. Her life had reached its end. She could barely function, much less reason.

The cold, stark bridge gave her little protection from the iciness around her. She was beyond freezing. She was almost beyond caring – almost. Suddenly the desire to get up and move gripped her. Dying next to the Moskva River was not what she wished. Maybe her final outcome would be decided by fate. But maybe she could have a choice in how she would die. She would be glad of that. Glad that she had not left everything to fate.

Pulling her weary body into an upright position, she began to drag herself through the thick pile of snow that surrounded her. Progress was slow – so very, very slow. She put one foot gingerly on the snow bank in front of her, her well-worn boots giving virtually no protection at all from the cold. Her body was so tired. So absolutely weary. The snow shuffled beneath her foot and repositioned itself neatly on the frozen surface of the river. Her hands froze, her gloves were useless. The snow bank reared up in front of her and she nearly fell. This was almost too much for her to bear.

She took another slow step and more snow fell gently below her. Painstakingly she moved up the embankment. Too weary to brush the snow from her face, she pulled herself further and further up the snow bank, pausing often to gasp some air into her lungs. The piercing cold bit into her hands. If it was at all possible, it felt as if the dark night had deepened.

And then, almost too suddenly it seemed, she managed to drag her weary body over the top of the snow bank. But the deserted streets offered no congratulatory crowds to appreciate her monumental feat.

The icy wind slapped her hard in the face and grabbed the breath from her lungs. She gasped. The cold pierced her very body with its long steely fingers and tried to rob her of her life. It seemed to pull her in all directions while she cried out in pain. The weeks of hunting for food in soup kitchens and begging for scraps outside restaurants, and the utter strength she needed for survival in these arctic conditions, finally took its toll.

She fell where she stood. The snow quietly covered her face in a silent show of victory. Slowly the cold ceased to bother her any more. She closed her eyes, pleased that the struggle was finally over.

* * *

The soft pale shadow of an approaching car's headlights fell onto the half-submerged body wrapped in a blanket of delicate, white, cruel snow. The driver hesitated a fraction of a second before making his decision. The car came to a sudden halt, but the engine kept running. The sound of a door opening and closing sliced the silence of the night with a clear, crisp, concise snap. The tall, silhouetted figure of a youngish man stood next to the car for a moment, and surveyed his surroundings. All seemed quiet and peaceful. Cautiously he walked over to the body and bent down to examine his find. As if in some sort of slow motion his black leather glove moved the thin layer of snow away from her frozen face.

He smiled to himself in amazement. She was still alive! It seemed almost impossible, but here she was, alive! The very same young woman he had been searching for ever since he arrived back in Moscow, twenty-four hours ago. He realised, though, that she was precariously close to death, and if he wanted her to survive, then he had to move quickly.

Lifting her gently into his arms, he returned to his car. She had lost so much weight that it was scarcely an effort to pick her up. The muscles in his face were contorted slightly as the guilt of what he had done to her hit home. Shaking his head as if to cast off the demons, he rationalised to himself that he could not have helped what had happened; it was not his fault. But still a speck of guilt remained hidden in his subconscious, gnawing away at him gently. He had learnt, on most occasions, to keep his emotions under control. But try as he might to forget the danger he had put this woman in, he could not. He was, after all, ultimately responsible. And that he found a bitter pill to swallow.

His deep, dark, fur hat cast a slight shadow over his face and his dark full-length coat swirled around his heavy snow boots. The scar that he had recently acquired ran softly down one side of his face. It was not an ugly scar, but it was noticeable.

He put his bundle gently down in the snow next to his car while he opened the door, all the while hoping that it was not too late. He needed her, this young woman. He needed her for two reasons. One was the fact that she had information that he wanted. It was unfortunate that it was the necessity for this information that had led to her present predicament. And, he needed her because he hated failure.

Bending down, he picked up the quiet, still form of the girl and placed her in the back seat. The warmth that radiated out of the interior of the car felt like a safe and welcome buffer against the outside world.

Getting into the driver's seat, he began to move carefully off, looking behind him to see if there was any traffic coming. But the night was silent. Even the moon seemed to have disappeared. The street lights shone onto the snow-filled road and he could clearly make out the indentations of cars that had followed this path earlier in the evening. Their tyre tracks had churned up the underlying mud and there were now two lanes of dark, slushy, dirty snow.

He drove along the deserted road for about five minutes and then, finally turned right into the light traffic heading towards St. Basil's. As he passed the cathedral he couldn't help but admire, as he always did, its stark beauty reflected against the lonely night sky.

Suddenly his eyes were filled with the blue flashing lights of the GAI, the Russian Police, just ahead of him and he was forced to slow down. There were seldom so many of them out in cold weather like this, especially all in one spot. Something must have moved them into action. Passing the Kremlin, he kept his head down and moved the car gently between the traffic that had now slowed to a virtual standstill because of the GAI. If ever the phrase 'a sitting duck' was appropriate, this was it. Could he trust them if he was stopped? He doubted it. There were not many people he could trust at this stage.

The car in front of him was pulled over and the GAI surrounded it. His car was next. He swallowed the rising bile in his throat, and a small bead of sweat broke out on his forehead and trickled down his face. What would he say about the girl wrapped up so harmlessly in the back seat? His story would have to be plausible. Old girlfriend? Drunk a little too much? Yes, that would be best. But could he carry it off? That was the important bit. Would they believe him? He swallowed again and felt the saliva fill his mouth. His breathing was shallow. Shit! This was all he needed.

Suddenly the GAI moved again, as if in one fluent motion. They advanced towards him, their weapons raised. One of them turned his head to bark out orders to those behind him. They surrounded his car. His window was banged on with such force that he feared the glass would be shattered. Their flashing lights filled the interior of his car like blue from a magic paint pot. He had no idea if they knew what he had been up to. No idea how much information had filtered through the ranks. Did they know about the girl? Was this it? Did they know about him? Would they just haul him out of the car and kill them both? His hand shook ever so slightly as he leant forward to open his window. He didn't have much choice at the moment.

Just as his hand reached the lever, the GAI frantically indicated for him to move on. He froze for a second, unsure of what to do next. One of the GAI looked at him from under his fur hat and indicated once more for him to move on. This time he seemed agitated, as if he wanted rid of him and his car.

He needed no further encouragement and drove on quickly. In his rear-view mirror he saw them pounce on the car behind and drag the driver out onto the frozen road. What would happen to him he neither wanted to know, nor cared. He had been lucky and he breathed an audible sigh of relief.

What he was doing was not actually illegal, but the thought of being stopped and having to answer questions that, at this moment, he himself didn't understand was just a hassle that he could do without. If they had recognised him, that would have been a disaster. And then, of course, if you could not answer their questions to their satisfaction it would mean instant jail, incarceration into the infamous Lyubyanka prison. This would be a hazardous experience, and he wished to avoid it at all costs.

The car skidded slightly on the loosely scattered snow that lay spread out on the road but he was almost unaware of it. His mind was a million miles away as thoughts raced furiously around each other in his mind, trying to get his attention. As he drove, he tried to piece together what had gone wrong. But the puzzle's pieces just did not seem to fit. Eventually he sighed, a deep long sigh, almost as if he was cleansing his thoughts. Once again, his mind focused on the young woman in the back seat.

His journey continued past frozen trees and frostbitten buildings. Fifteen minutes later he pulled into a hidden side street and through a pair of iron gates that had almost rusted off their hinges. Glancing to his right, he saw the familiar sight of the security guard idly twisting his baton to and fro. He had made a point of getting to know the security guard as one never knew when one might need someone to look out for you, someone to warn you of unwanted visitors.

He knew that if he carried a woman out of his car there would be no problem; only a nudge and a wink. The following day he would be met with a sly nod and a handshake, to be followed by a sigh which would proclaim that, as a married man, he couldn't indulge in the pleasures that his friend seemed to take for granted.

He parked his car and put off the lights. Removing his

gloves, he gently blew onto his hands. By God, it was freezing tonight! Putting his gloves back on, he looked cautiously into his mirror. This place was one of a few hide-outs that he had in the city. His hair rose slightly on the nape of his neck, almost in anticipation of danger, and his eyes darted cautiously from side to side as he looked around at his surroundings. Was it safe to get out of the car? The quiet of the night surrounded him and engulfed him in her arms. Yes, he finally decided, it was safe.

This was the best chance that he had. He hoped that the girl was still alive – she hadn't stirred since he'd put her in the car. If she was dead, then he'd have to finally accept failure, but that wouldn't be easy to do. Not after so long. Not after so much planning.

With a frown, he got out of the car and looked cautiously around him. He opened the passenger car door, reached in and pulled the young woman over to him. The security guard appeared to be buried in his paper and after an initial glance in his direction, didn't bother himself further. Pushing the door closed, he leant against it and readjusted his bundle. With the girl over one shoulder and one hand in his coat pocket he moved quickly across the snow. The girl wasn't heavy. A mere featherweight, and he was a strong man. Reaching the front door to his apartment block, he punched in the code and went in, pushing the heavy cream-coloured steel doors aside. They closed silently behind him as he entered the familiar passage.

The passage was ill-lit and the stench of urine hit him hard after the fresh air. He reached the rickety steel lift cage. Once inside, he put a cold finger on the rather dirty-looking button for the third floor and pushed hard. The lift clambered up in a very trying manner. It was very old and he was sure that at any time it was going to pack up.

Reaching his floor, the door of the lift opened noisily. The light was a bit better just by his door. He had seen to that when he had first moved in as he hadn't wanted any nasty surprises.

As he reached his apartment he tried to keep hold of his bundle while he fumbled in his coat pocket for the keys. Behind him he heard the lift move back down. Unlocking his front door, he stepped cautiously inside.

Before he had gone out earlier in the evening, he had placed a thin thread of cream cotton from one side of the door to the other, almost touching the cream carpet, if anyone entered, it would be broken.

Looking down, he saw the slight thread was still intact. Stepping gently over it, he breathed a deep sigh of relief and he began to believe that luck was finally smiling down on him.

Without taking off his heavily snow-covered boots, he moved directly to the spare room where he put the girl gently down on the bed and removed her meagre, dirty clothes. He felt no male surging within him, just a feeling of pity and shame. Shame that he had inadvertently done this to this girl.

She was so desperately thin. Her bones showed clearly through her dirty skin and her breasts had almost dissipated in her waif-like form.

Now came the tricky bit. Could he save her? Quickly he put the warm thick pyjamas on her that he had grabbed from the cabinet next to the bed. Dashing to the bathroom, he removed an aluminum bag from his first aid kit, and slipped her inside its warmth. Hopefully that would do the trick. Taking off his boots and outer garments, he returned to the front door and discarded them in a crumpled heap on the floor, to be picked up later when he had more time. But his gloves he put in a nearby drawer.

Settling down next to the bed in a spare chair, he rubbed his hands over his arms to warm himself, and waited. He had left the heating on, but it was very poor in the older Russian flats. If you happened to live on the lower floors, as he did, the heating proved ineffective at times, but should you live on the top floors of the apartment blocks, then you would find it unbearably hot. It always took him some time to warm up when coming in from the freezing cold outside.

The hours ticked tediously by. He looked at his watch and watched as the second hand slowly progressed around its face. Slowly the minute hand would move onward and upwards and then, finally, the hour would change. He got up from his comfortable chair as he feared he might fall asleep, and stretched his aching muscles. Thoughtfully he parted the heavy dark green curtains and peered out of the window, glancing idly around. He hoped that he had not wasted his time. If she died after all, that would be disastrous. He had to know what she knew.

He returned once more to his chair and made himself comfortable. Leaving a small side light on, he got out a magazine from the table next to the chair and began flicking unseeingly through the pages. He sat like that for what seemed an age, only moving to get up to get himself a glass of vodka and to go to the toilet, and occasionally to change his reading matter. Falling asleep was not an option. Not yet. Not now. He had to know if she would live, and if she did, then maybe this niggling guilt that had been plaguing him for the last few weeks would disappear.

Hours later, he began to see the start of a change in her. He wasn't too sure if he was imagining things at first, but slowly he noticed the colour returning to her cheeks. Life was beginning to stake its claim on her body, whether she wanted it to or not. She was going to live.

To prevent her overheating, he removed the blanket and tucked her up under the thick quilt that was on the bed. Now he could sleep. He dragged his bone-weary body into the passage and closed the bedroom door behind him. Thinking it safer to lock the door as he didn't want her to wake up frightened and leave while he slept, he locked the door and pocketed the key. He stumbled sleepily down the dark passage and into the main room, where he collapsed onto his big double bed, into a dreamless encounter with the unknown.

The first rays of sunlight penetrated the murky mists around him and plucked Patrick victoriously from his dreamstate. Making his way into the bathroom, he took a quick shower and put on a pair of clean, neatly ironed jeans and T-shirt. He then went to the front door, where he picked up his discarded coat and scarves and hung them up on the coat rack, together with his hat.

Moving quietly to the spare room, he unlocked the door. The girl was still sleeping soundly. He realised with a start that even though she was half starved, she was still the beautiful girl he knew. The girl he had found crying along the roadside one day after the matron at the school had given her a particularly hard beating. He had marched right into the school and told them that the teenager would now be living with his family. True to his word, he had dropped her off with his aunt and uncle, and that is where she had remained. And when they died, he had fetched her and got her a job and a small apartment in Moscow. He of course knew that she would jump at the chance to help him should he ask, and he did ask. It was just so unfortunate that things had gone this way.

The natural light from the sun added a quality of innocence and purity to the young woman. However, her face was dirty and she had obviously not had a bath in a long time. But beneath the grime her features were extraordinary, something that he had always admired about her. She had high cheekbones and full red lips, which were now blistered from the cold but should soon heal. Her naturally wavy hair was a deep auburn and it lay spread out beneath her head on the pillow. The contrast between her hair and the white of the pillowcase was an artist's dream.

She looked malnourished, but that was hardly surprising. People were dying everywhere in Russia at the moment. If it wasn't the cold that claimed them, it was the lack of food. This was nothing new in the regions, but to Muscovites it was a new and unwelcome experience. Something they preferred to ignore, or brush off as one would an annoying fly.

It was late afternoon when the girl finally stirred. She felt warm and luxurious for the first time in ages. She had to be dead, she thought to herself contently, as only Heaven could feel this good. No more cold – it was wonderful not to feel cold any more. Slowly she turned her head and knew that she was dead, because there, sitting next to her, was Patrick. She blinked and opened her eyes again. No, she definitely wasn't dead. And he looked very, very real.

His blond hair shone in the sun and he looked like a smaller version of Arnold Schwarzenegger, the movie star who had won numerous body building competitions in his past. Blue eyes stared back at her and she looked back directly into them. After all, what had she to fear? Nothing or everything. The scar running down his cheek was new though. She knew this because it hadn't been there the last time she had seen him. When he had come to her asking for her help. That afternoon, too had been cold. But not once did she think of refusing him. She had loved him deeply, ever since he saved her. It felt at times that he was always her protecting angel, and he had never let her down until now. But he had to have a good excuse, she hoped.

She watched idly as he kept touching his scar as if wondering how it had actually got there in the first place. It didn't, however, distract anything from him, but instead added to his beauty.

He cleared his throat. 'You must be hungry?' She watched

mesmerised as he rubbed his hand once more down his clean-shaven cheek to check, abstractedly, on his scar.

She smiled, nodding quiet assent, and suddenly she felt the bubbles of laughter rising up from deep within her. Hungry? She was half starved! He got up from his chintz covered chair and left the room. Returning shortly, he put a tray of soup and bread on the small table next to her bed, which she eyed eagerly. Half sitting up, she ate greedily. It had been a long time since she felt so totally saturated with food. The soup dripped down her chin and she wiped it with a blue napkin that Patrick handed to her. She smiled, fulfilled.

After she finished eating, she put the empty bowl back down on the table next to her, feeling stronger and less vulnerable now that she had food inside her. Turning to face him she said accusingly, 'Where were you? I waited for two weeks. Two weeks, Patrick!'

Her soft, gentle voice brought with it a tremendous sense of guilt that he tried to swallow. He bent down next to the bed, took her hand in his and looked directly into her eyes. 'God, I'm sorry, Natasha. I tried.' He squeezed her hand tighter. 'You have to believe me, I tried. But I couldn't get back into Moscow before yesterday, and I just prayed you would still be there for me.' He breathed deeply. 'Still waiting as we agreed.' Even to his own ears his excuse sounded feeble and weak. What would she make of it? he wondered to himself.

She looked into his eyes and hers filled with tears. She did believe him. She didn't know why, but she did, even though it felt like a bitter pill to swallow. It would take a lot for her to forget what she had had to go through these past few weeks to survive. The scrounging, the cold, the petrifying fear. Not being able to go back to her lovely little flat that she had decorated with such pride. Not being able to draw money from her bank account in case she was found and killed.

Death had been so close. She closed her eyes and he withdrew his hand from hers. 'You're tired. I'll let you get some sleep now and we can talk later.' She nodded. She was very tired, in fact she felt totally and utterly physically and emotionally exhausted, but she had to give him the piece of paper that she had found.

'Wait, Patrick,' she called after his retreating figure. 'If you look in the pocket of my coat you will find a copy of part of a document that you asked me to search for.' He paused, looking back at her with an unreadable expression on his face. 'I found it for you, Patrick,' she finished quietly lying back against the bed.

He removed the empty bowls of food from the room and returned them to the small white, neat kitchen. He quickly gave them a wash and put them on the side to dry. Once he had finished this small task, he checked up on her. She lay huddled, buried deep beneath the quilt, fast asleep, and he quietly closed her bedroom door again. He fetched her threadbare coat and searched in the pockets, pulling out the bit of information that had nearly cost her her life. Reading it with interest, he exhaled sharply. Who would have thought it?

A little while later he left the apartment and made his way down the stairs to the ground floor. He opted for the stairs and not the lift as he felt restless and he had a lot to think about. When he opened the main door a blast of freezing cold air slapped him with force across his face, and he gasped for a moment as he caught his breath. The sun was now beginning to disappear and he glanced at his watch. Three-thirty. Pulling his coat collar up, he reached into his pocket and pulled out a packet of cigarettes. He paused and surveyed his surroundings, casually lighting a cigarette, and walked unhurriedly through the main gates.

Once he was out of the main gates he leant against a tree and breathed in deeply on his cigarette. Exhaling a small trail of smoke, he idly watched some girls jumping up to reach the lowest branches of the trees to shake snow onto each other. He saw them laugh and chase each other, envying their joviality, innocence and youth. Things he had had once, a long time ago, before events took control of his life. He could only shake his head at his naivety.

Throwing his cigarette down in the snow, he watched as it sizzled out, making a tiny pool of water. He moved forward slowly and carefully. Occasionally he turned, as if to glance up at the sky. He was aware of everything that surrounded him, and nothing escaped his sharp glance, not a sound or sudden movement.

His rendezvous was the lake at the Novospassk Monastery. When he arrived he watched as a handful of energetic strutters ran or walked around the lake, trying to catch the last of the sun.

Looking across the lake, he saw him straight away: an old man sitting huddled in his grey coat casually stroking a dog. Joining the strutters, he circled the frozen lake twice, before glancing curiously once more at the man's dog. It could not possibly be his dog, because he knew that the old man was a loner, someone who indulged in his solace. But he wasn't about to ask questions. He walked slowly and unhurriedly through the snow and sat down on the bench next to the old man.

He didn't look at him, but stared straight ahead. Barely moving his lips he murmured, 'I found her – the girl.'

The old man coughed 'You're damn lucky, Patrick, damn lucky.'

'I know, and I have some startling information that she managed to get for me that you won't believe. Someone at the Embassy was very careless, and undoubtedly when their error is discovered their head will roll.' He got up and stretched and then casually walked on, amongst the families and children who had suddenly descended to enjoy the thrill of the frozen lake. In the middle of the lake sat a few fishermen who had drilled their obligatory holes in the snow, hoping for the elusive fish.

He didn't glance back or make any sign. It appeared to passers-by exactly as he wanted: that a young man had sat briefly next to an old man with a dog and had patted the dog. Nothing sinister there at all. Burying his face in the collar of his coat, he smiled to himself. It was dark now, but nothing could dampen his mood. By a chance in a million he had found Natasha again, alive. And he was extremely thankful for that as he now had information to bring down a government.

He smiled selfishly to himself as he walked slowly back to his flat, making his plans.

3

The wrinkled old man smiled pensively to himself and bent forward awkwardly, as the stiffness in his back seemed to be getting worse, and stroked the dog with a large, gnarled hand. Patrick had been wrong in assuming that the dog wasn't his, it was. After he'd paid a small contribution to the animal welfare organisation, the local shelter had given him the dog. It wasn't a really big dog, more the size of a bull terrier, but it was a real bastard of a dog as you could see no clear line of breeding through the friendly animal. His bedraggled wisp of a tail wagged gently to and fro, quietly tossing a few new snow flakes around, and he looked up at the old man with affection in his dark, molten eyes. 'There must be at least ten breeds of dog in you,' he whispered to the animal, who continued to look at him with worship in his eyes. The old man rubbed the dog's fluffy white ears, and smiled softly to himself as he patted his brown splodged body.

'Did you like our man Patrick?' he asked the dog in a raspy confidential whisper. It was a general question. One that didn't really mean much, but filled the empty silence around them. The dog got up hastily and wagged his tail furiously. 'When I'm tired of you I'm going to put a bullet through your brain. What do you think of that, hey?' The dog was now so excited it was jumping up and down next to him. 'Oh! All right, let's be on our way then.' Rising slowly to his feet, as the pain of arthritis worked through his legs, he began to walk in the direction of his home. He smiled to himself: 'his home'. He liked the sound of that. His small bit of sanctuary in the madness around him that had at times seemed almost suffocating.

He nodded to two elderly women who were just passing by, taking their nightly constitutional. They had wrapped themselves up tightly in their fur coats and hats and just glared at him. Oh well, he thought, you can't win them all. He walked cautiously over the icy paths, trying to avoid a fall. His boots were in good condition, which was in total contrast to his rather sad worn old coat. But both still managed to keep most of the cold at bay. The night had closed in and darkness surrounded him, with just the occasional street lamp giving off a weak indication of light.

As he walked, his mind wandered to thoughts of Patrick and found it hard to believe that it had been ten years since all this began. He was, of course, much younger then and Patrick was a mere child in his eyes. In those days he had had just a twinge of the onset of arthritis, nothing as crippling as what he experienced now.

They had both been sent to Donnas, the capital of The New Independent State of Commans, a new state that had been created out of the old through a violent and rather predictable revolution. They had both been idealists, and had recently left their jobs at the Moscow university where they had taught Russian history. Firm friends, together they had huddled in the cold, dark nights, heads bent over a bottle of Russian vodka, trying to put their idealism into practice and attempting, somehow, to make something good out of bad. It was during one particular drunken and philosophical night that they had swooped on the idea of applying to the Russian government for a job abroad. And, much to their enormous surprise, they had been successful.

When word had come through a few months later that

there was a job for them both in Commans, they had jumped at the chance, their eagerness contagious. Neither had given much thought to what they would actually be doing, and it was this naivety that would, ultimately, lead to a lack of respect for their government and their subsequent deviation from their chosen path.

Their job had been to monitor the situation in Commans for any sign of major interest by another government in that area, and to report back to the Russian government. The new independent state was situated between South Africa and Zimbabwe, and it had vast areas of mineral wealth that the Russian government were eager to exploit, and primarily keep for themselves. Their task was simple: find out what they could about who was interested, infiltrate where they could, and bring back as much information as possible. The Russians wanted to be sure of their position before making their move.

The Russian government had no intention of governing Commans, but they did want its wealth, which was extensive. The Russians knew, as did a few other western powers, that the people of Commans could be easily incited to create instability. Once instability was achieved, then they could move in with their investments and so reap the rewards that the country had to offer, without actually contributing much in return. The Commans would once again return to a state of poverty which no one really cared about. Interest was only being shown now because of the rich platinum and diamond fields that had recently been uncovered, and once those were stripped, interest would wane.

It was here that they had first stumbled on an underground movement with international connections simply called the Yellow and the Red. It was an unexpected find, but it held enormous implications. This was a serious organisation involving financial backing by more than one country. The aim of this group was to destabilise the country once again, sooner than expected and it could be done very easily after the recent revolution. The general consensus amongst the members of the Yellow and the Red was much the same as that of the Russians: to strip the country of its natural mineral wealth. But after that their plans deviated, with the Yellow and Red wishing to gain ultimate control of the country, and, of course, to put themselves in as leaders.

They promised the people wealth and stability and vast rewards for believing in them. None of which they had any intention of delivering. Once in power, they planned to give the president absolute rule, which would justifiably keep them in power for years to come, and their people in subjection. The Russians and other western powers were delighted to find this group of wayward thinkers, consisting, primarily, of treason offenders recently released from prison. It would be easier to manipulate a situation that was already in existence and so, indirectly, line their pockets.

The old man paused as he walked along the Moskva River away from the Kremlin, and tried to catch his breath. His age was beginning to catch up with him and he found himself tiring easily now.

The dog looked up at the friendly old wrinkled face beside him. Soft white hair was scattered around his chin and upper lip, which were slowly being covered in snow. 'It's all right old fella, I'm just a bit cold.' He breathed deeply and painfully, leaning one gnarled gloved hand against the rough surface of the wall to steady himself. 'I'll be OK in a just a jiffy,' he wheezed. The dog's tail wagged in acknowledgement and he sat down to wait. The old man cupped his hand over his nose and mouth so that he could draw one or two deep breaths of the warmness that his own air made. Ah! That felt better. As his foot took one step in the snow after the other, he watched as the tiny flakes scattered from his boots and remembered what it had been like to walk in the dry sand of the desert around Donnas. What warmth. How he longed for just some of it at this moment.

He could still taste the wonderful beer, Castle, that they had been able to purchase there for next to nothing. Reaching deep into his pocket he pulled out a bottle of vodka and took a deep swig. As it flowed through his veins, it warmed him and he smiled to himself.

His thoughts returned once more to Donnas. Although they had known about the Yellow and Red and were making great strides in acquiring the knowledge that they sought, they were still taken by surprise by the suddenness of the uprising. Nothing had prepared them for that. Both Patrick and he had been caught with their pants down, literally. The first thing that they had known about it was massive shoutings in the street. They had both jumped out of bed, virtually simultaneously, and he remembered how he had nearly passed out with the sudden rush of blood from his head. Although it had been early in the morning, many people were up already. In Africa, when the sun gets up, so do the people.

It was not usual for them to have stayed together, but they had entered the country on the pretext of tourism and as there was still so much confusion after the recent uprising, no one was paying particular attention to any newcomers. They were too busy trying to keep their grasp on power.

They had been lucky and had found an apartment quite easily in the centre of the rather dilapidated capital. It was small and quite rickety, and at times they wondered if it would stand the test of time. They shared a bathroom and toilet with the tenants of the other four rooms on their floor. It wasn't a very big apartment block, just four floors, and they were on the second. There were wooden floors and walls, with a slanting tin roof. In one corner they had a small hob-nob stove where they could make simple meals and boil some water for tea.

The wooden floors were covered with loose multi-coloured floor mats that complemented the deep colour of the wooden floorboards. They each had their own bedroom, which had been scantily furnished with a single bed each and a small table and closet for their clothes. Over the beds were colourful blankets that added a sense of surrealism to the place.

The apartment block contained a mixed bunch of people. Some worked for the Red Cross, some were students and some, like them, professed to be holiday-makers.

Their small sitting room had one big window with old broken wooden shutters that had been painted blue at some time, as was evident from the badly peeling paint. It overlooked the small African market, which, although dusty and a bit run-down, had been adequate for their needs, supplying them with fresh fruit and veg daily.

Suddenly there had been a mad shout in the corridor and Anne Greeves – he winced slightly as he recalled her panicked look – had flung open their door that fateful morning. None of the rooms had keys to lock them so it was not surprising that she could just fling the door open. Her long, dark, straight hair was barely combed and her clothes had been thrown on rather haphazardly over her wiry five-foot-six frame.

A few minutes before, she had been looking out of her dusty window which faced in the opposite direction to their apartment. She had heard them before she had seen them, and for a moment had been unsure what she was hearing, but it had soon become terrifyingly clear: the quiet tread of thousands of people walking in their direction. Then she had seen them – tiny specks of heads bobbing up and down as they walked. It was then that her colleague had barged into her room and stammered that they had to get out of there; she had been told that there was a bus waiting downstairs to take the Red Cross workers away from the building immediately.

Anne had gone straight to warn her friends, and now the frightened deep blue eyes of this young and innocent girl looked at them. 'You've got to hurry. There are thousands of people on their way here, and the last and only bus out of here is leaving now! Hurry, for Pete's sake!' She was shaking with a desperate fear, and with fluttering and agitated hands tried to convey a sense of urgency.

They had hurried, and as they ran down the rickety old steps on the outside of their building, they saw, just beyond the bus, what appeared to be a massive sea of black faces, all marching with a purpose.

The bus was moving already, but thankfully it was slow as it wound its way through the market place and they managed to catch up with it, and fling themselves on board. Once through the market it would be able to go quicker. In the distance they could already hear shots being fired and shouts coming from behind them, mainly from those who had decided to stay to protect their things, and those who had not been lucky enough to catch a bus. They passed the army heading back in the direction from which they had come, their heavy tanks churning up dust and sending them swerving onto the edge of the road.

But they were safe – huddled together on the floor of this dirty bus, with far too many others than would normally be considered safe. The ride was awful, and they found themselves being knocked around as the bus swayed from side to side as it gathered speed out of the town. It was hot and the stench of baked sand and sweat soon became overwhelming. All around them sat innocent people, people who had already been through too much and seen too much suffering and were also desperate to avoid the impending conflict instigated by the Yellow and the Red. And behind the Yellow and the Red stood the shadowy figures of governments who didn't want their involvement known. But in a short time, they would arrive – in force, probably as a peace-keeping team. And they would begin to rebuild the country with the sole aim of stripping it of its value. The saddest bit of all would be that the world would just watch as people died and governments got rich.

The cold was getting more biting and he glanced idly at the driver of a car. The man was just staring aimlessly at the snow in front of him as he drove, his reflection suddenly illuminated eerily by a passing car.

It brought back what he had seen on Patrick's face that day. When he had turned to look at him, he had visibly started. He remembered the fear he had felt. The fear of not wanting to look, not wanting to know what Patrick saw. Dreading it. In fact he did not want to be sitting there amongst more than twenty others, none of them daring to breathe or utter a word. Fear gripped them all, and he was just plain terrified. He was no hero; there had been no choice. If they had stayed, they would have been dead, of that he was certain. You do not face a sea of armed people. They had known about a new uprising, but the enormity and suddenness of it had surprised them and taken them off-guard.

The old man swallowed and realised that he could still taste that fear in the back of his throat, even today. The pain of a terrible sadness and loss cut through him and he paused once more to catch an agonisingly slow breath.

In the end pure instinct kicked in and he followed Patricks gaze – then wished with all his might that he hadn't. There, sitting tightly bundled by two big African women was Anne. There was no doubt that she was dead. She was pale and her eyes stared straight ahead. Dead eyes. He watched mesmerised as Patrick began to worm himself painfully along the floor of the bus between a sea of people, trying to reach Anne. And he saw the pain etch right across his face like a streak of lightning when he reached her. He was unable to take his eyes off Patrick and stared blankly at his futile attempts to bring Anne back to life. In the end, Patrick just sat there, holding Anne close to him, rocking her back and forth, back and forth, for hours.

Patrick and Anne had become very good friends during their time in Donnas and the unfairness of it all began to tear him apart. The bullet that had killed her had gone straight into her back. And suddenly he saw it almost as if it was taking on a force and personality of its own, the blood that flowed freely from Anne's fatal wound. Oozing between Patrick's fingers, it made them gel together in one horrific bundle of red pus.

Those around her had been too dazed to notice – let alone care. They themselves had already lost too much.

He would never forget Patrick's face, and he knew without a doubt that that memory was one that Patrick would carry with him to his grave. He knew that Patrick would feel responsible for her death until the day he died. Because they had known what had been planned. They could have warned her – told her to get out. But they did not know when, and that was what they had been working on when it all came down around their ears. They could have saved her. This young woman – out here in Africa trying to help those less fortunate than herself – one more innocent casualty of war.

The old man reached his apartment and slowly began to punch in his door code with stiff, cold fingers. He had not known that he had been crying, but against his cheeks ran two tiny rivers of ice. She had been so young and so beautiful and so caring.

Opening the door, he went in, then closed it gently behind him.

4

Natasha awoke slowly the following morning to the smell of fried bacon. Lazily she reached her arms above her head and relished the enjoyable, warm, luxurious stretch. Her body wallowed in the total abandonment of the moment. She glanced around, noticing the cream coloured walls and carpet. It really was a lovely room, and warm – warm – warm! She wanted to shout it from the rooftops!

Although she and Patrick had a long standing friendship, she had never, until now, been privy to his apartment. The thick, heavy dark green curtains that must have been opened earlier hung neatly on either side of the huge windows to let in as much light as possible. She loved the multi-coloured quilt that covered her bed. Reaching over for the towel that Patrick had thoughtfully left for her on the nearby chintz chair, she noticed her pyjamas for the first time. They were covered in huge teddy bears and rabbits. Running her hand over them, she laughed out loud. How strange life was.

Throwing aside the quilt, she lazily drew herself up into a sitting position. Her toes splayed out with the luxurious feel of the carpet. She got up and stood for a while gazing out of the window. The snow lay thick and heavy on the ground. There was a tree right outside the window whose branches seemed to be buckling under its deluge of fresh snow. Down in the street she saw an old woman all bundled in brown: brown fur coat, brown hat, brown shoes. She even glimpsed a pair of thick brown socks. She had no boots, and poverty screamed out from every fibre of her being. In front of her she pushed an old rusted wheelbarrow with a few mangled-looking potatoes. Natasha sighed, knowing the feeling of desperation that this old woman must be feeling only too well. The poor were everywhere now. Communism had collapsed in favour of the idealisms of the West. But with it came the extremities in wealth. Now more than ever Russia had some very rich and a huge number of very poor. Everything that the West had to offer did not always glitter with gold.

Carefully opening her bedroom door she noticed Patrick in the kitchen just opposite. He nodded her in the direction of the bathroom. Turning left, her feet sank into the plushness of the passage carpet. It was a beautiful deep green. The first door on the right was partially open and she pushed it further, to reveal a blue bathroom. Although small it was quite adequate. Closing the door, she walked over to the blue bath and turned on the taps. Warm water flowed out freely, filling it virtually to the brim.

Putting her fluffy green towel down, she looked around for some shampoo and bubble bath, then climbed into the bath and began to soak away the grime and dirt that she had accumulated over the last few weeks. She washed herself and her hair, then let the water out and refilled the bath to the brim again. After adding some more bubble bath, she lay there and began to think about her life and the fact that a short while ago she had almost been dead. And here she was, happy to be alive.

Once more back in her room, she opened the cupboard and rummaged through the clothes that she found there. They were adequate, but nothing special. Pulling out a pair of light blue jeans, she looked for a top to match. This she found in a nice white woollen jersey. The clothes were a bit too big on her, but what did she care?

There was a tap on the door and Patrick poked his head round. 'Finished?'

'Almost.' She reached for a nearby comb and slowly started to disentangle the knots in her hair. It always frustrated her trying to get them out. Patrick watched as she pulled at her hair, trying to make sense of the mess that it had become. Putting the comb down, she turned to him. 'Ready.'

She followed him as he led the way back down the passage, past the bathroom and his bedroom, to the lounge. It, too, had lovely big windows that overlooked a small frozen park and the colour scheme matched the green of the passage walls beautifully. The couches were done in a light cream with a tiny thread of gold running through them. The floor was the same colour as the passage, with a Persian rug thrown over it. In one corner stood his computer, which he had obviously just been working on, as an unfinished document could be seen on the screen.

'Please, have some bacon.' He indicated the small coffee table in the middle of the room.

She sniffed gleefully at the warm, welcoming smell of freshly cooked food. 'Bacon!' she whispered. 'How did you know that that was just what I felt like?'

He smiled slowly to himself as he watched her snatch at it eagerly and start to devour the long-forgotten delicacy. He sat down next to her, frowning slightly. 'How are you feeling today?' he asked protectively.

With her mouth full and her lips lightly coated with grease from the bacon, she nodded and mumbled, 'Great – good.' Suddenly she stopped chewing and looked him directly in the eyes. 'Thank you.'

'For what?' He stirred, feeling slightly uncomfortable with the direction that the conversation was now taking.

'For not leaving me there to die.'

He leant towards her and, taking her lips with his, kissed her fully on the mouth. Pulling slightly away he said softly, almost ashamedly, 'I am just so sorry that it couldn't have been sooner.' He stood up and looked down at her. She looked back and licked her full red lips. Her mind was beginning to work once more. Did she really believe what he had told her? If he was telling the truth then there would be no problem, but just a very small part of her was beginning to have some doubts. But why would she doubt him now? Why? He had looked after and protected her for so long. She shook her head ever so slightly as if to shake off the memory of a ghost.

She had always loved him, ever since they had met. But did he love her? She didn't know. But then why the kiss?

'I'm sorry, Natasha, I didn't mean to do that.' He turned in frustration from her and stood staring out of the window. He felt her confused eyes on him and shoved his fists deeper into his jeans pockets. He was angry at himself for letting his lust get the better of him for one split second. He vowed that he would never let that happen again. Ever.

'I know,' she said. 'I know you don't love me, but you did find me. And,' she bent her head down and hesitatingly added almost in a whisper, 'I love you enough for both of us.'

He turned to her almost in fury and gripped her shoulders. 'Enough! This nonsense must stop!'

She shuddered beneath his sudden violent outburst and watched as he stormed out of the room. Why was he so angry? she wondered to herself. He had looked after her for so long, why was he angry now?

Natasha stood up, no longer hungry, and silently put her hand over her mouth as her eyes filled with pain and tears. She stood like that for a long time, gazing silently out of the window at the bleak landscape in front of her, not seeing or hearing. Please let him be telling me the truth, I could not bear it if he had left me there to die on purpose, she prayed silently. The niggling doubt began to erase her fragile trust.

She started when she felt Patrick's presence behind her.

'I'm so sorry, Natasha, but I just can't.' He turned her to face him and saw the tears in her eyes. 'Dammit, don't you understand?'

She avoided his gaze and looked down at her toes. 'Yes, I think I do Patrick. I understand very well,' she lied, sounding convincing even to her own ears. She sighed and returned to the couch, where she finished eating her bacon. He cared, but he didn't love her. And where that left her, she did not know. They had had a past together. He her protector, always – until now. From the day that he took pity on this poor orphan girl, he had never let her down. He had found her her first job and helped her with a flat. She *had* always trusted him, and within a short space of time she had fallen head over heels in love with him. And that was probably why, if she was honest with herself, she found herself in the predicament that she was in now. It had been her inability to say 'no' to him, abandoning her instincts and trusting *him* instead of herself. But he had never let her down – until now. And the crux of the matter was simply that she could be dead, and it would have been his fault.

Patrick and Natasha sat on the couch in the lounge, each nursing their own cup of tea, dwelling on their own thoughts. The tension had abated slightly, but there was still a small element of distrust, mainly on Natasha's side. Patrick sat staring into his cup, oblivious of his surroundings, mulling over the very recent and rather shocking information he had got from Natasha. The sunlight bounced off Natasha's hair, adding a brilliant sparkle to her eyes, but Patrick didn't notice. How was he going to explain to her why he had taken so long to reappear? How could he explain without giving too much away? Frowning in consternation, he looked absentmindedly into his now ice-cold tea. Taking a sip, he barely noticed the thin layer of skin formed by the milk until it slid uncomfortably down his throat. Cringing at the ghastly taste in his mouth, he put his cup down on the side-table, deciding not to risk drinking any more.

Getting up, he walked to the window, thrusting his well-manicured hands into the back pockets of his jeans. Suddenly he seemed to reach a decision and turned to her. 'Natasha?'

She put her cup down on the table next to her, almost in slow motion. Slowly she raised her eyes to meet his. 'Yes Patrick?' She wondered what he was going to say, not sure yet if she could trust what would come out of his mouth.

'I *am* sorry, you know,' and he added almost absently, 'I'm sorry to have let you down like that.' She sat very still, watching him, noticing the slight flickering of his eyelids and the twitching of a small muscle in the side of his cheek. Suddenly it felt as if the whole room was overwhelmed with unanswered questions and deceit. It was almost screaming out to her to ask him something, but what? What was she supposed to ask him, this man whom she had trusted with her life on more than one occasion? This man whom she had worshipped and looked up to? She was missing something here but she did not know what. Slowly she lowered her head and looked at the floor, and asked so quietly Patrick had to step slightly towards her to hear what she was saying 'Why didn't you come, Patrick?'

She heard him clear his throat and could almost sense his despair. 'I was detained at Heathrow.' He paused, as if trying to formulate his plan. 'Someone planted something on me and it took a while for me to get it sorted out.' He remembered how he had sat there, across from the interrogation officer, repeating over and over again that he had no idea how the small packet of heroin had been put in his bag. The questions just went on and on, as he sat at a small wooden desk on a rather rickety wooden chair.

He remembered the stench of fear and dread that had filled that dark, dingy room. His interrogator was a young man of about thirty, obviously desperate for some form of recognition, and in Patrick he sensed rewards, if only he could get him to confess to being a heavy-duty drug smuggler. But Patrick was not into drugs. It took two weeks before the idiot had finally called the number that Patrick had given him, and Patrick watched with glee as he saw his interrogator's smile disappear. He was released almost immediately after that, but without an apology.

But what he could not have foreseen were the difficulties that Natasha would get into. When he had left Moscow, everything was falling into place. Natasha had the job that he wanted her to have and she was getting the information to him that he needed. If he had known what would happen, he would have tried harder to get out quicker, or he would have made damn sure that he did not land in this predicament in the first place. He reflected bemusedly that hindsight was a wonderful thing.

Natasha still looked down at a small speck on the carpet. As she looked she noticed that it didn't quite match the rest of the floor. Funny, that. She shook her head and sighed. Could she believe him? She wanted to – desperately. Looking up, she watched his stony face as it stared out of the window, and saw the muscle twitching just below the scar. He sounded sincere, but then he hadn't really told her much, had he?

She spoke slowly, as if to emphasise her words. 'OK – maybe it is best if we forget everything and go our separate ways.' She was testing him.

He turned, stunned. 'No! No, Natasha – not now.' He spoke almost desperately and came over to her, gripping her arms as he knelt on the carpet before her. 'No – we can't stop now. We've come too far. Please don't do this,' he begged.

She looked down at him in some confusion. Her instinct screamed out at her to get the hell out of this mess as soon as she possibly could. Against her better judgement she bent her head towards his and whispered, 'All right, we'll do it your way.' Hearing the audible sigh of relief that passed through his taut lips, she could have kicked herself for giving in so easily, but if truth be told she felt that she had no choice. Not at the moment, at any rate, but later – maybe.

He had been too good to her for too long, having saved her from more than one sticky situation, and she would not let him down, no matter what the personal cost to her would be.

He lifted his head and looked her straight in the eyes. 'Thank you, Natasha. Thank you.' Releasing her hands, he got up and stood in front of her. 'There is someone that I would like you to meet.' He had watched her carefully as her mind worked. She had become too valuable to him and he had no intention of letting her out of his clutches.

She nodded. Whatever was to begin – had now begun.

Ten minutes later, they found themselves outside in the snow, all bundled up in their furs, walking towards his car. He had lent her one of his coats, which was a good thing as hers was a bit threadbare. For a moment her thoughts drifted back to her cosy, warm, *nice* flat. Yes, she had liked her flat very much. She could picture in her mind's eye her pride and joy, the one item of luxury that she had saved for what seemed an age, a really expensive, luxurious warm fur coat. If she had had that with her when things had gone awry then she would have stood a better chance against the elements.

In the distance she heard a small bird call. She looked around idly, trying to find it. Eyeing the stone apartment building next to them, she noticed that the same big stone bricks that adorned the lower half of the apartment also surrounded the parking square that they were now in. Looking up to the roof, she saw a man knocking the ice off. This had to be done regularly in winter as the ice formed sharp sheaths down the side of the building and once they got to heavy, they would plummet to earth with brute force and could kill someone. And then, of course, when it heated up and the ice melted, the roofs would flood.

The sun shone brightly and she had to cover her eyes with her gloves as she looked up at him. Then she noticed it, the sudden silence. She could not say exactly when she noticed it, or what made her notice it, but she did. She looked from one roof to the next in slow motion. It too had a man on the roof knocking the ice off.

She turned slowly from one to the other, noticing that they had both stopped what they had been doing and were looking, not at their work, but at *them.* 'I'm just going to get into the car and start the engine to warm it up before I scrape the ice and snow off,' Patrick said to her. She nodded absently and stood quietly next to the car.

The shrill cry of a bird echoed through the still morning air and as she turned, her gaze met that of the security guard. He stood there, smiling to himself, as he leant on the wall of his security box – and she froze.

As she watched him she heard Patrick get into the car and start the engine. It faltered on his first try, and suddenly it all made sense. Her heart stopped, briefly, and then she ran and ran as fast as she could. Behind her she heard Patrick start the car again and suddenly an explosion ripped through the air. The force of it threw her to the ground and blood slowly started to ooze out of her, soaking the white snow around her.

And then there was an eerie silence.

5

John Masters tossed and turned as the fever raged through him, his dark hair plastered to his forehead with sweat. He had managed to drag himself into work at the British Embassy that morning and had even managed to do three interviews for visas, all of which he had refused. But when the fourth one was presented to him he began to falter as his cold changed into full-blown flu. Handing the fourth visa request over to a concerned colleague, he took the subway home and then tossed himself promptly into bed.

It wasn't like him to be so ill and he had to admit that he missed his girlfriend's gentle touch, but their ways had parted a few months ago and she had returned to Sweden. They'd had a good time together but in the end they had both decided to call it quits. He had heard via the grapevine that she already had someone else in tow and was three months pregnant. That bit surprised him as she had never wanted kids with him. In fact he wouldn't have minded having kids, but in the beginning they were just having so much fun together, and near the end of their relationship they seemed more like brother and sister than red-hot lovers.

'Oh God!' he felt awful. Moaning, he rolled over, trying to dull the pain in his stomach.

He had arrived in Moscow almost two years ago and was enjoying the experience very much. He loved the people, and the job had proven very interesting with hard, busy summer months and less taxing winters. He had integrated himself with the locals and was a firm favourite amongst his peers as he was a hard worker and extremely conscientious, as well as good-looking.

It was no good, he could no longer ignore the nausea and dashed to the toilet. Returning a few minutes later to his room, he collapsed once more into a comatose state, feeling just plain awful.

The phone woke him a few hours later, buzzing softly next to his ear. He had to answer it in case it was important.

'Hello?' He sounded groggy even to his own ears.

'I am really sorry to worry when you are so ill, John,' came the soft sound of Elizabeth's voice on the other end of the phone.

'That's OK. What's up?' He had always liked the leggy blonde.

'This is just a call-down to let you know that there has been a minor car explosion outside one of the apartments just a few kilometres east of you.' It was common practice now that if anything major occurred like a bomb blast, there would be a call-down to notify all members of staff. It was a procedure that worked well and kept everyone informed on developments, which helped if they were to get a call from worried relatives back home.

'Thanks, Elizabeth.' He ran his hand over his forehead, feeling the heat.

'No worries. I know you're ill, so I'll call Ian for you. Now get some rest and see you back at work soon!'

'Thanks again.' He replaced the receiver with a small smile on his face. Yes, he liked her very much, and when he was better he might just get around to asking her out. And on that note, he fell fast asleep.

6

The special Russian intelligence agency, the FSB, received a call two days later and, surprisingly enough, this call was actually diverted correctly and put straight through to Nikolai Sebislav's office. As one of the so-called 'top guns' of the FSB, it was unusual that a call would come directly to him. Picking up the phone, he listened, frowning, took one or two notes with his new fountain pen, nodded once more, then put the phone down. He sat like that for a while, beginning to think. Then tapping his pen in an agitated manner on the desk, he punched the intercom button and bellowed for his secretary. He might as well have done without the intercom because she could hear him loud and clear through the thick wooden door. He was a very arrogant man.

Olga entered the room in a graceful manner. Her gracefulness was only added to by her cool light-grey trousers and the thin white blouse that revealed a little bit of white lace underneath it. She was oblivious to the admiring gaze from Nikolai, whose eyes travelled from the top of her five-foot-eight slim frame to the bottom of her neatly polished grey shoes. Like many Russian women, she had an exquisite face with high cheekbones. Her blonde hair fell neatly in a bob around her face and her green eyes shone bright and clear.

Her voice when it came was pure music to his troubled

soul and for a moment he almost forgot what he had called her in for. 'Yes, Nikolai?' she asked, a shade irritated at having her filing interrupted.

'Sit,' he ordered, trying to recollect his wondering thoughts, and in so doing softened his order by adding, 'please.'

She sat down neatly opposite him with her legs crossed at her ankles and looked at him with her head tilted to one side. He watched silently as she ran her moist red tongue over her fading pink lipstick. Clearing his throat rather harshly, he rose, agitated once more, and walked over to the small window. He noticed, absently, how the green paint was slowly peeling. Unconsciously his fingers played in the gathering paint flecks that lay scattered at the bottom of the window frame.

He watched as two snow flakes fell gently together, only to melt as soon as they touched the outside of his window. The drop of water they formed ran gently down the window leaving a trail. He followed the trail automatically with his finger, leaving slight brown streaks behind on the window. Still looking out of the window, he asked her, 'When last did you hear from Patrick Smith?'

His voice gave nothing away. She watched his back muscles flinch slightly underneath his pale cream shirt as he asked the question, and noticed the slight trail of dirt that his short stocky fingers left behind on the window. Turning, he looked at her. She had gone pale. 'Why do you ask?' There was a slight tremor to her voice that did not go unnoticed.

Walking back to his desk, he slouched once more in his black leather chair. Although it was torn on one side, it was still extremely comfortable and he loved it. He sat down and looked at her with a hard, searching look. 'I know about you and Patrick, and now is not the time to be playing games with me,' he added softly, running his stubby fingers over his grey facial hair. 'I have neither the time nor the patience, for that matter.'

He watched her closely and under his intense scrutiny she buckled slightly, closing her eyes briefly. She had long dark eyelashes. What Nikolai was referring to was just pure sex between her and Patrick. There was no love on Patrick's part – just a need that she was willing to fulfil. She was fond of him and enjoyed his passionate lovemaking, but that was all there was to it. And besides, she hadn't seen him for quite some time now.

Lifting her head, she looked directly at Nikolai. 'He's dead, isn't he?' Her voice seemed to fill the room and bounce off the walls.

'Yes, he's dead.' The answer was clear and left no room for doubt. Nikolai rubbed his fingers agitatedly through his coarse grey hair.

To her surprise, she found her lip trembling slightly. Quickly she bit down hard to stop it. What was wrong with her? she wondered. 'Are you sure?' she asked. She had no idea why she was feeling like this. It was perhaps the thought of his beautiful, alive body being no more.

'As sure as we can be.' Seeing her pale face, he cleared his throat, feeling a bit unsure of how to proceed. He need not have worried.

'He came to see me about three months ago.' She looked directly at Nikolai, but her mind and thoughts were elsewhere. She was remembering how he had banged on her door, and how, when she had let him in, he had entered with a sense of urgency and desperation – almost as if he had reached the end of his tether. He had grabbed her as soon as he crossed the threshold and smothered her with hard, needy kisses. And she had responded. After all, was she not a woman as desperate for sex as any normal male?

He had picked her up and with one foot closed the door behind him. Taking her straight through to the bedroom, he had hungrily devoured her, ripping her clothes off and barely waited for her to be ready before placing his hard, erect penis inside her.

There had been an added urgency to his lovemaking which had almost overwhelmed her, and afterwards he had lain next to her and lit a cigarette. She, in turn, had pulled the sheet up to cover her naked breasts and sat next to him with her back resting against the headboard. Theirs was not a 'cuddle after sex' relationship. It was just pure sex.

'Did he say anything to you?' Nikolai's voice brought her thoughts shrieking back to the present.

She smiled a slow, sad smile. 'No Nikolai.' She sighed softly to herself. 'Talking was not an important part of our relationship.'

He nodded as if he understood far more about her relationship than she did. And then she knew that the FSB had not hesitated to bug her apartment as well. She accepted this as she accepted most things in Russia.

'Is there anything else that you need from me?'

'No.' He paused, abstracted. 'Nothing.' He wasn't looking at her when she quietly got up and crossed to the door. She gave him an enquiring look as she opened the door and then closed it gently behind her. She leaned against the hard wood of the door for a few seconds, her thoughts far away. Slowly she straightened herself and walked over to her desk, as efficient as ever.

Nikolai left his office a few minutes later, feeling disgruntled. He had to try and clear his head. He found solace in a small, somewhat dilapidated park across the way from his cold grey building. Putting one snow-covered boot carefully and precisely in front of the other, he walked, his mind a million miles away. He went over and over the same things again and again and none of it seemed to make any sense. Once or twice he glanced up sharply as if he had heard an unusual noise, or as if he sensed another presence. But it was nothing more than the snow falling off the branches of the many frozen trees that surrounded him.

At this moment, it appeared as if there was no one in the park besides himself, but judging by the snow-encased muddy footprints that he followed as he walked around the same circle, that had not been the case earlier in the day.

Hours later, and just as the sun was making a futile, feeble attempt at warmth, he returned to his office. Sitting down in his chair, he slammed his fist down on the table. 'Damn the man!' Kicking his heavy snowboots off but leaving his coat on for the moment, he covered his eyes with his hands. He sat like that for a good ten minutes, and then suddenly sat up, 'Of course! How silly I have been!' he almost shouted to himself, hastily removing his coat in his excitement.

He grabbed the phone and smiled to himself, and into his mind's eye came the clear image of his counterpart in London, Robert Brown – a man he liked and admired. They had spent a couple of months together in Oxford as students many years ago when they had both been studying political science. It had only been on Nikolai's return to Russia that he had decided to join the FSB, or the KGB as it was then known. But he had always kept himself up to date with regard to Robert's progress in MI6, which had never for a moment been in doubt.

Putting a call through to MI6 in London was more complicated than just phoning direct. First he phoned the British Embassy in Moscow and spoke to one of the MI6 operatives that he knew. He stressed the importance of his call and she agreed to meet him within half an hour in a designated park about ten kilometres from the FSB building.

He saw her as soon as he arrived. She was sitting quietly on a bench facing a small frozen pond. Her blonde hair was captured in her fur hat, but a few tendrils had escaped to tease her face. He watched as she brushed them irritatedly away with a gloved hand.

'Hello, Elizabeth.' He sat down quietly next to her.

Her grey eyes met his dark ones and she smiled. 'Hello Nikolai.' They sat like that for a while, each looking quietly at the frozen pond. Its brightness hurt his eyes and he rubbed them.

Elizabeth broke the silence first. 'What's so important?' She looked into his troubled face. He spoke slowly and to the point. He spoke of the bomb attack and explained why it was so important that he speak to his old friend Robert Brown, in MI6.

She nodded. 'I'll arrange it.' She stood up, bundling her dark fur coat more closely around her, and walked confidently off. A short while later, Nikolai got up and returned to his office to wait for the call that he knew would come.

It was dark when the phone finally rang. Nikolai had not bothered to put on any lights, but had just sat there, waiting. He did not answer it straight away but waited for the fourth ring. Slowly he lifted the cold receiver to his ear. He spoke – then listened. Robert's voice came clearly over the phone, 'I'll see what I can do, Nikolai. Give me half an hour and I'll get back to you.' He paused as if to add something else, but thought better of it.

The light from the street lamp just outside his window poured across Nikolai's desk. As he replaced the receiver he sat staring idly at the patterns that the light created across his desk, wondering bemusedly why he had never noticed them before. Finally he shook himself free of his thoughts, gathered his coat and boots together and left the office, feeling more assured about the situation that he found himself in. But still, in the back of his mind, niggled a gnawing doubt of unrealistic proportion.

* * *

Robert Brown replaced the receiver at his end, and twisting his luxury leather swivel chair around, looked out of the window over the River Thames, casting an idle look over the Parliament buildings. Hmm, he thought to himself, I will have to move quickly on this one. Damn awkward timing as well.

It took one call for him to get the permission he needed, and two hours later he was on a flight out of Heathrow, heading for Moscow with a forged passport that contained a Russian visa. He always kept a supply of forged passports that contained various visas for just such an emergency. It was just part of the job.

The movie on the flight was a recent James Bond film and Robert had to smile to himself. He was as far removed from the looks of James Bond as you could imagine. He was tall and wiry, with a balding head and a small pot belly. His eyes were of a nondescript grey and he was clean shaven. He enjoyed the movie, however, and a small part of him wished it was like that in real life. He wouldn't mind the gorgeous girls throwing themselves at him. No, he wouldn't mind that at all. Slowly he drifted off to sleep.

His plane arrived fifteen minutes late and skidded slightly sideways on the icy runway as it landed. As he had very little hand luggage with him, he was one of the first to disembark. The queue for passport control was long and it took a while for him to reach the desk. He presented his passport and looked straight at the passport control officer. Having presented many false passports during his time in the office, he knew it would not help to look nervous. The passport officer was in no hurry. Robert had time to notice the white flecks from the man's greasy hair that had fallen onto his collar. On his cheek was a huge yellow pus-filled pimple that seemed about to burst. Robert cringed slightly as, finally, a big hairy paw with filthy nails returned his passport to him.

Gingerly he took the passport, wishing he could douse it with antiseptic, and walked towards the luggage carousel. Because of the delay in clearing passport control, his small black case had already been taken off and put neatly on one side with the rest of the passenger's luggage from his flight. He left the airport in search of a taxi. The freezing air that met him as he stepped out of the airport building wrenched the air out of his lungs and he gasped loudly, taken unawares. Hailing a taxi, he asked to be taken to the small Russian restaurant where Nikolai had suggested they meet.

During the hour's ride to the restaurant, Robert glanced out of the window at the icy fields and snow covered trees and buildings. It was bleak, stark and cold. Shivering, he leant forward and asked the taxi driver to turn up the heating.

Finally he arrived at his destination and looked with slight dismay at the grey stone building that presented itself to him. Seeing three doors of equal size in front of him, and no sign of a name anywhere, he bent his head towards the taxi driver, who was just giving him change, to ask where the restaurant was. The driver smiled and indicated to some stone steps that led downwards. Thanking him, Robert picked up his case and made his way gingerly down the frozen steps, holding onto the short, rickety iron rail with his left hand.

Once he reached the nondescript door, he pushed it open quietly. Inside was dark and it took a moment or two for his eyes to adjust. In one corner was a small fire burning and he looked around at the pleasantly decorated restaurant. Soft lights lined the dark wooden tables, each with a small green shade. All the tables were still deserted so he was either early or late for lunch. He glanced at his watch and decided that he was late.

The chairs were decorated in patchy red and black shapes with the occasional dollop of white and yellow thrown in.

The floor was made up of red stone tiles. The smells that attacked his nostrils were to die for, and his stomach grumbled in approval. A waiter dressed in tight black pants and an almost impossibly crisp white shirt came to ask if he could help. When Robert mentioned that he was here to meet Nikolai, the waiter ushered him quietly and discreetly into a small private back room.

Closing the door behind him, the waiter withdrew. Robert walked towards Nikolai, who had risen, and they gave each other a warm hug. The years had taken their toll on Nikolai, he noticed. Gone was the dark hair, but unlike himself Nikolai had retained a thick bush of grey hair. His moustache, was still there, and had also turned grey. He was dwarfed by Robert's six-foot-three frame.

'Thank you for coming so quickly, Robert.' His accent was thick and heavy.

'No problem. It's good to see you again, my friend.' Robert avoided Nikolai's gaze. A move which did not go entirely unnoticed by Nikolai.

'Sit. Let's order something to eat.'

Robert sat down opposite Nikolai. The room that they were in was small, with its own little fire in the corner. There was only room for the one table, but it could have seated four. A small mat lay across half of the stone tiles that lined the floor and a thick, heavy, ruby red curtain hung against one wall. As they were below the level of the street, Robert assumed correctly that there was no window behind it at all, merely an illusion of one. The lighting in here was dim, but the fire added warmth and light, helping to make it cosy. They enjoyed a nice quiet meal while reminiscing about the times they had shared during their time in Oxford.

The chairs were big and comfortable and soon Robert began to relax. It was only when the order for coffee had been placed that Nikolai reached down beside him and pulled out a small brown leather briefcase. Moving aside some of the cutlery and crockery that they had been using, he placed it down in front of him on the white tablecloth and opened the small gold catches. Reaching inside, he pulled out a paper folder, put his briefcase once more on the floor and pushed the folder across to Robert.

Robert sat looking at it for a few seconds before, hesitantly, reaching for it. Putting one well-manicured hand on top of the file, he gingerly opened it. The first document in the folder was a photo of the remains of a car bomb. There was not much left of the car. The photos that followed showed the damage that the bomb had caused to the surrounding area. Finally Robert looked across at Nikolai, who himself reached for the photos, which he placed upwards on the table in front of Robert.

Indicating the photos depicting the car, Nikolai said, 'The remains found in this car were the remains of one Patrick Smith alias Charles Newman, one of your agents, I believe.' He cast a sly glance at Robert as he said this. Robert said nothing, but Nikolai observed his small, sudden intake of breath. Robert, clearing his throat slightly, looked across at Nikolai, not saying a word. But Nikolai did not need him to say a word; he knew that what he had said had hit home. He laughed quietly. 'Yes, we knew he was a double agent. We've known for a long time. But,' he continued quietly, 'did you?'

Robert nodded. 'Yes, we knew.'

But somehow Nikolai wasn't too sure if he had, in fact, known. But that was not actually his concern. He continued to look at the photos and his small feeling of victory passed as he frowned and said, 'There was a girl with him, but we haven't been able to identify her yet.' He felt, personally, as if that was a small failure on his part and it galled him to have to admit defeat to Robert.

'So he was with someone else when he was killed?'

Nikolai nodded, abstractedly. 'Yes, it looks that way, I'm afraid, and we really have no idea who she is…' He left the sentence unfinished, almost as if he was waiting for Robert to fill in the blanks.

Robert was trying, successfully this time, not to let his emotions betray him. Damn Nikolai and his element of surprise! His own thoughts began to work. Had the two just been mere acquaintances? Was it, after all, important? He rather thought that it was. He looked up and Nikolai looked back at him. The air dripped with unspoken tension. What the hell was going on here? He just hoped that he would be able to keep one or two things quiet and hoped fervently that Nikolai wouldn't be able to work them out for himself. At least not until he could get things sorted. He had to move quickly and quietly.

Nikolai rose. 'Come on, let's go and look at the bomb scene, then I can take you to your hotel.'

'Why would I want to see a scene that has obviously been gone over with a fine tooth comb by your boys?' Robert queried, beginning to feel slightly weary. His shoulders were beginning to burn with tension but he dared not put a hand on them to rub them. Under no circumstances could he let Nikolai know how concerned he was.

'Good point, but I thought that you might like to get an idea of the scene surrounding the explosion. As you mentioned, there is virtually nothing left now at the scene, except a big hole in the tar where the car was.' Nikolai sounded matter of fact.

Robert frowned to himself, trying to put two and two together. There was no real need for him to go out to the site, but obviously Nikolai thought it would be a good idea. But why? He swallowed heavily and avoided Nikolai's gaze. 'All right. As you say, it might be a good idea for me to get some insight into what took place.' But even to his own ears, his voice sounded unconvinced.

They finished their coffee and put on their coats and hats. Robert followed Nikolai out of the building. On reaching the pavement outside, Nikolai raised his arm and a driver and car appeared. Robert's case was put in the boot and they both clambered into the back seat.

Nikolai barked instructions to the driver and they were soon on their way. Their path took them past the Kremlin and along the Moskva River. Turning to Nikolai he asked curiously, 'How deep does the river freeze to?'

'I'm not really sure. But it should be more than one metre. On some of the lakes around here, you will find people taking their cars across, so it must be frozen to quite a depth. But I'm no expert my friend.'

Robert shivered and wrapped himself up more tightly against the cold.

'Why do you ask?' Nikolai raised his eyebrows curiously.

'My son is studying geography at university and I am finding myself more and more interested in what he is learning,' Robert continued, 'so it is purely curiosity on my part.'

Nikolai nodded. 'Yes, one's children get one interested in some strange things.' He looked out of the car window and into the distance, wondering silently to himself.

Arriving at the bomb scene, they both got out and Nikolai indicated the obvious destruction of the building and the area which had been cornered off with thick red tape. The tape now lay broken in places, still attached to various poles, and the wind picked up the various sections and tossed them lamely in the air. The place where the car had stood was covered in snow and Robert, reflecting on the photos that he had just seen, mentally made a note of where the exact damage that the car bomb had done to the tarmac was.

The car itself had been removed shortly after the explosion. There was not much to be learnt here now, and after a freezing twenty minutes they piled themselves back in the car and headed towards Robert's hotel, and some degree of warmth.

* * *

He couldn't tell when the nightmare began. He was only conscious of a deep foreboding as it unfolded deep within his mind, almost like a gigantic tidal wave engulfing everything in its wake.

'Stop!' a man's voice shouted. 'Stop! Please help me! I beg you!' There was a razor's edge to the man's pathetic cries. 'Help me – *please*!'

What the hell was going on? A sense of overwhelming panic gripped Robert. There was something wrong here, but what? He turned to face the sound of the voice, but he couldn't find anyone. It was dark and he was alone, standing under a bright, fluorescent green light that somehow shone red. Frantically he started searching, emptying boxes and rummaging through clothes and old vegetables. He was on the dockside somewhere and he felt wet as it began to rain. Pausing to listen, he realised that the voice had stopped, and then someone touched him on the shoulder. He turned icy, a drip of terror running down his spine. Suddenly a scream filled the air and waves started to crash in on him from all sides and it got even darker, but the green light seemed fixed on him and he was unable to escape its menacing bright red tentacles.

He was stuck on a small piece of sand with a steep grey sand-filled embankment to his left. The water kept coming and he began to splutter. He was drowning and still none of it made sense. Each wave that hit him smashed into his face seeming to carry a message of confusion and frustration that made him writhe in silent agony.

He woke, startled and spluttering and sat up in bed, sweating. Hastily he put on the small broken lamp next to his bed. A circle of light lit up the room around him. He lay quietly in the big double bed and looked unseeingly at the unremarkable picture of a flower on the opposite wall.

Throwing off the heavy blankets that he had so eagerly wrapped himself up in earlier, he walked over to the mini-bar and pulled out a bottle of water. He noticed that the water was not cold, so the fridge was obviously not working. Opening the top, he thrust it aside and began to gulp greedily at the cool refreshing liquid. Then he turned to the window and pulled back the horrible brown curtains, which were the only real offending article in his room, and a big, fat brown egg-infested cockroach fell onto his hand, causing him to start suddenly. Tossing it hastily onto the floor, he quickly reached across for his boot and slammed it into him, killing it instantly. He climbed back into bed and looked at his watch. Seven-thirty. Just time for him to shower and order room service. Reaching across for the phone list, he dialled the number and ordered his breakfast. They promised that it would be with him in ten minutes, which was perfect as he could get up and shower and dress before it arrived.

True to their word, breakfast arrived ten minutes later, just as he was fastening the last button on his shirt. Opening the door, the maid put the tray down on a small yellow table. Thanking her, he quietly closed the door behind her. He ate with relish as he was starving. When he had finished he fetched his boots. He was just finishing with the laces when there was a knock on the door.

It was no surprise to see Nikolai standing there when he opened the door, as they had arranged this meeting the previous evening.

'Good morning, friend! How are you today?' Nikolai looked refreshed

'I'm fine thanks, Nikolai.' Nikolai followed him back into the room as he picked up his coat, which he had left lying across the back of one of the chairs, and his wallet from the table.

'Good – good, there is a lot of work that I need to show you today. Are you ready?' There was a slight questioning tone in the usual brusque manner, almost as if he wasn't quite sure of himself.

'Yes, let's go,' muttered Robert as he flung his coat on and walked with Nikolai towards the door.

Robert closed the door behind him and the cockroach, which had feigned death until now, started to move. He smirked to himself and knew that by tonight there would be twenty of them. Victory, for today at least, was his.

7

The old man opened the crumpled paper that he had borrowed from his neighbour, scarcely noticing the ink marks that were coming off on his fingers and blending in with his yellow stained digits.

He was sitting, huddled, in his damp, dingy kitchen near the small stove that he had put on, trying to absorb its miserable ray of heat as the central heating was poor and inadequate. A small moth-eaten woollen blanket of interwoven colour covered his old, bent legs. The dull yellow chairs were old, and the legs of the table were uneven. The whole room seemed brown and drab, with the depressing weather outside only adding to the already dispirited atmosphere.

The paper didn't seem to hold much interest and he was pleased that he hadn't wasted what little money he had on buying his own copy. He slowly scanned page after page, using his finger as a ruler, and in the process smudging the ink slightly until some of the words ran into the others. He was getting slightly bored.

It was the second to last column on the third to last page that suddenly made him stop and re-read what he had just read. Could it be possible? For a moment he couldn't breathe. He gasped for air and began to choke. Bending over the paper, he coughed and coughed until finally, with a tremendous struggle, he managed to regain his breath.

Shaking, he re-read the article twice, the words scorching themselves on his brain and making him feel very afraid.

'Unknown man and woman killed in a bomb blast ... no suspects ... no clue ...'

An ice-cold drop of sweat ran down his hunched back and he began to shake. It had to have been an ambush! But why hadn't Patrick been aware of it? Why? He had surely been extra cautious after picking up Natasha? He had to have been! 'Oh dear Heaven!' he mumbled stiffly to himself. He rubbed his forehead with a trembling hand, trying to make sense of things, and in so doing left behind some faint black marks from the newspaper. His reasoning failed him, but he also knew instinctively that if Patrick was dead, then it was almost a certainty that he would soon be dead also. Their lives had been too intertwined for it to be any different.

Closing the paper, he abstractedly folded it and unfolded it a dozen times before placing it neatly on the old table in front of him. Silently he looked down at the dog which was lying as usual by his feet. Sensing the old man's gaze, the dog looked up at him and tilted his head enquiringly to one side. Gently the old man reached down to quietly stroke the dog's ear. The dog enjoyed the attention and rubbed his face against the arthritic hand that was giving him so much pleasure.

The old man knew that he didn't have much time left if he wanted to live. He would have to move quickly, but he was old, and tired. Tired of the whole sordid business. It would actually be a relief to finally put an end to it all.

So he just sat there, listening to the ticking of the wall clock, which had been hung on a dodgy nail sticking through the stained brown wallpaper. An hour ticked by, then two. His dog, who had been trying to get him to go for a walk, finally gave up and made his way into the small hall. He listened to its nails scratching on the wooden floor as he walked across the creaking boards, then heard him settle down in the corner where he had laid out a meagre blanket for him.

And then he heard it: a small, silent, almost non-existent noise at first. He listened more closely and then he heard the noise again. The dog moved slightly and gave a small whine. Then nothing. And the old man knew. He knew without a doubt that he was sitting within the shadow of death.

Death arrived in his kitchen wearing gloves, which were neatly placed on the old man's shoulders, squeezing them slightly. He shivered and muttered, without turning to face him, 'I've been expecting you.'

There was a cruel, mad laugh, and the hands were removed from his shoulder. 'Have you now?' A small rumble of laughter followed. 'Well, I definitely will give you more credit than poor old soppy Patrick!' Death stood in front of him and gloated. 'He was so concerned for himself that not once was he aware that I was there, that I *knew – knew what he had done to me!* He had absolutely no idea – poor, *dead, pathetic* Patrick!' He spat out the name venomously. 'You will all pay for what you have done to me! All of you!'

Turning abruptly from the sitting figure, he walked across to the almost bare cupboard and took out a glass. From the rusty-looking taps, he filled it with murky water for the old man. Then he took a small packet of white powder from his pocket, and added it to the water.

The old man watched but he still couldn't move. He didn't stand a chance of outrunning the man. So he sat and watched, almost fascinated by his own death.

The glass was placed on the table in front of him. 'Drink.' He watched as the deadly crystals dissolved in the water. Slowly one rose to the surface and burped out loud, before sinking back down to the bottom.

Death leant over him and he could smell the faint aroma of cherries on his breath, 'Come on, drink.' And then he continued in a gentle voice, as if coaxing a child, 'This will really make it easier for you.' He laughed cruelly, and added almost as if it was an afterthought, 'Such a pity that none of you thought the same for me, when you destroyed my life. So I am *pleased* – no, that isn't quite the right word.' He hesitated as he rubbed his fingers under his chin. 'I am *honoured* – yes, that is the right word – I am honoured that I am able to provide an easy death for you.' He leant forward once more and looked right into the old man's eyes. 'Of course it won't be as explosive ...' he left the sentence unfinished.

And, as if in slow motion, the old man held out his hand for the glass. Raising it to his mouth, he drank as if in a trance. And while he drank he listened to the ramblings of a half-sane man. 'I am not killing you for any other reason than revenge, you must know that.' He walked away and leant against the far wall, eyeing the old man. Then he sighed as he reached into his coat pocket and took out a cherry. He glanced at it before popping it into his mouth. Slowly twisting it around with his tongue, he located the pip and spat it out on the floor. There it lay, all wobbly and with bits of cherry still stuck to it, staring up at him.

'You and Patrick took something so precious away from me that I could never forgive you.' He suddenly seemed quite sad. 'And it has taken me a long time to work things out and plan.' He threw his fist down on the table as if to emphasise his own words. 'Plan, plan, *plan*!' And he added quietly as he took the glass away from the old man's dead fingers. 'Now you are all going to die. You are all going to feel the pain that I have felt.' His voice trailed off. 'And only then will I have peace.'

The gloved hand threw the glass on the floor with some force and watched as it shattered into dozens of tiny pieces. Sighing, he gave one last glance at the dead man, and nowhere in his body could he drum up an ounce of guilt or sorrow for what he had done. As far as he was concerned, the old man had paid the price for his crime. On his way out, he kicked the still form of the dog.

8

It was a beautiful, tranquil, warm night in northern South Africa. What the locals would refer to as 'balmy'. The heavens seemed to be decorated with a thousand stars and the potent fragrances of dusty earth and intoxicating flowers filled the air.

Stuart Love looked out over the screaming audience from behind the small partition next to the platform. Taking a deep breath, he mustered his courage and ran out onto the stage, getting ready to belt out his first song. It was a type of rock ballad and it had just hit No.1 in the US and No.2 in the UK. Here in South Africa it was still a fairly new song, but by the sound of the crowd's response they were loving it. So it would not be a surprise to anyone if it made No.1 in South Africa in a few weeks.

He was performing at the Sun City superbowl for the first time as part of his world tour. The Sun City complex had been formed after an enterprising young man flew over the empty landscape pointed to an area and declared that it was here that they would build a hotel and resort, the likes of which South Africa had never seen. And so it was. It comprised hotels, gambling, a wave pool, golf course, lake – you name it, it had all been thought of.

During the apartheid years, Stuart would not have felt comfortable touring South Africa, but with the end of apartheid he had been very excited at the prospect. It really was a beautiful country with lovely people, and his only regret was that he had not come out here sooner.

As he jumped up in the air and ran around the stage in his tight black leather pants and white gypsy style shirt, the audience went wild with excitement. This was the part that he loved. The music flowed through his veins on a wonderful night like tonight. He fed off the exhilaration of the crowd, which gave him more speed, more agility and more energy. He could at times get so carried away with his enjoyment of a gig that he would not notice how exhausted he was, until he virtually collapsed at the end of his performance.

He grinned a wide, white toothed smile at the keyboard player, and Len grinned back. There was feeling here tonight, and it was incredible. He really admired Len's magic on the keyboard and it looked as if Len was really enjoying himself. He did four songs of fast tempo following quickly one after another, until his dark, wavy hair stuck to his forehead with a warm mixture of sweat and dirt. The sweat ran into his eyes and he swept it off with the back of his hand. The lights on the stage were getting hot and he was relieved when Sad Sam, their charismatic guitarist, followed on with a solo of immense beauty.

This break enabled him to go off stage for a few minutes and down a pint of ice-cold water. He watched idly from a dark corner as the performance was played out on the wooden stage set up near the Valley of the Waves.

He could see that the guys were enjoying themselves as there were smiles all around as Benjamin Novis, their drummer, Len and Sam went wild with their instruments. They played two numbers, enabling Stuart to get his breath back. The third piece was quieter and served as the prelude to a song that Stuart never, ever left out.

As the music stilled, Stuart walked quietly back on and took centre stage, where a stool had been placed for him to sit on. The audience had grown quieter as if suspecting a mood change.

With a single spotlight on him, he began to talk quietly to those around him. 'This is my all-time favourite song.' He paused, as the crowd cheered, knowing that a favourite hit would soon be played. Stuart continued to speak, but more to the heavens than the souls that filled the audience in front of him.

'It was written about a girl I loved very much.' Another chorus of cheering and whistling went up, and he could see the small flickering of lights all around him as people held up their lighters or lit small candles.

Len hit the first note and the crowd cheered, recognising the popular love song. They soon joined in, swaying gently together. The song began and Stuart's beautiful Irish tones filled the air. He had the audience in the palm of his hand as he sang the final words:

How I loved thee, my beautiful Anne,
How I loved thee.
Too young to die.
And too beautiful to live.
I will always be here and you will always be there.
Goodbye, my darling Anne.
How I love thee, how I loved thee.

The spotlight vanished and the lights came, on leaving Stuart in the dark, while the rest of the band took the audience back up with louder, full voluptuous numbers.

Stuart reappeared two numbers later and the evening ended on a high note with the audience crying out for more and more. They just couldn't get enough. But after three additional songs, the band called it a day and walked off the stage for the final time.

'I'm knackered.' Len flung his guitar down. Getting from

the stage to their rooms hadn't been difficult at all. Sun City had provided extra security guards who saw them quickly and efficiently back to their suite at the Lost City. An African theme flowed easily from the four double en-suite bedrooms that joined the lounge. And it was in this lounge that they now congregated to discuss the evening's performances.

'Yeah, me too,' voiced Sam, who threw himself down next to the couch in which Len had sunk down. Len eyed him curiously, noticing that more grey was beginning to appear in his dark brown hair. Good, he thought to himself. It somehow made him feel better about his thinning mop of blond curls.

Benjamin, himself a full-bodied hulking mass of a redhead, looked from the very fair slight Len to the dark butch Sam and smiled to himself. 'They enjoyed it though,' he said, referring to the audience, and paused. 'Listen to that, they're still at it.' He grinned in great satisfaction. He loved being famous and he loved all the attention, especially the female attention. Sticking his chest out a bit more, he walked across to the window and looked down at the grass below.

Stuart sat quietly on a small green stool, leaning against the wall and surveyed his band members. They were all in leather tonight, but they had opted for various colours. Len had on yellow leather pants and a golden shirt with floppy sleeves. The colour did not actually suit him as it made him look paler than he actually was. Sam had chosen red leather and a red shirt with short-sleeves. It was a deep ruby red and added to his dark, stormy look. Benjamin was the only member of the band that was not clean shaven. He had a huge massive mountain of red hair growing across his face and he thoroughly enjoyed his new look. He was wearing navy blue leather pants topped with a shirt of multi-colours. This was typical of the loud, big, lovable redhead.

'What did you think, hey, Stu?' Benjamin asked, grabbing

a bottle of water off the table. He turned curiously to Stuart, 'Stu?'

Stuart shook out his long dark locks and eyed Benjamin. 'Yeah, Benjy?'

'You OK, mate?' Benjamin gulped down the cool liquid and replaced the empty bottle on the beautiful mahogany table that sat in the middle of the room.

'Yeah, I'll be fine in just a tick.' His dark eyelashes hid his beautiful blue eyes and Benjamin looked across at Len with a knowing look. The three of them had started the band together in a small pub in Dublin. Never in a million years had they expected it to be so successful. But that was five years ago now and they were doing extraordinarily well. Sad Sam had joined them after their first stint in a dingy nightclub in London and they had never looked back. His guitar playing was pure genius.

They had the usual arguments, but overall they were great friends and looked out for each other. They all knew the origins of Stuart's song about Anne. Sometimes when he sang the song, it would leave him emotionally drained. The frequency with which that happened now was getting less and less; but tonight, so close to where she had died, had obviously got to Stuart.

Anne was a girl he had been at school with whom he had hoped to marry one day. They had agreed to wait for a year while she fulfilled her life-long dream of working in Africa. She was lucky to get a job with the Red Cross. When she tearfully but excitedly bade Stuart farewell, neither realised that the farewell would be final.

They had been in London when news of her death reached them and Stuart had been inconsolable for days. And to make matters worse, her last letter arrived three days later, telling him what a wonderful time she was having and how she couldn't wait to see him again; how she was ready to settle down and have tons of kids with him!

She had been due to arrive two weeks later and join them on their final two-week stint in England. Then they were to be married. She praised him in her letter, saying that he was one in a million to let her go and experience a bit more of life before settling down. She added that she had lots more to tell him and couldn't wait to do so.

Stuart battled to come to terms with her death. At first he got himself drunk and seemed prepared to remain in that state for a while. And then, one morning Benjamin had come down to breakfast and found Stuart fast asleep across the breakfast table in their small apartment. Beside him were the lyrics and music of one of the most beautiful love songs he had ever heard.

The days had passed in a blur after that and in a way Stuart had seemed better. Almost as if he had eradicated some of the ghosts and demons that had almost driven him to dementia. But one is never truly free of one's memories.

The song had reached No. 1 in the UK and the USA and had remained there for two weeks. Whenever Stuart sang his song it often left him with a deep sadness that no one and nothing had been able to lighten over the years. Sometimes he was able to cover up his sadness a little better than at other times.

Unfortunately for him, his vulnerability added a certain appeal, and girls flocked to him wherever he was, swearing undying love and adulation.

As far as Benjamin knew, Stuart had not been with a woman since Anne and it was unlikely that he would, unless he loved her very, very much. The pain of loving Anne and then losing her had almost destroyed him and he was not yet ready to allow another love into his heart. He was not ready for the pain that came with loving.

9

The long-haul flight seemed just that – long and tedious – and for what seemed to be the hundredth time Sam got up from his seat. Sam did not like flying, and the only way he could control what he considered to be a weakness was to ask the stewardess a variety of questions: 'Can I have some more water? How far are we? Do we still have long to go' – this last question he had asked every ten minutes since departure and would continue to ask until they landed. The blonde stewardess smiled sweetly at him as he appeared once more in her galley. But at times like this, Sam was oblivious to any female charms, and he asked if he could have some more water. The stewardess reached behind her and opened a small door. 'Here you go.' She handed the bottle of water to the rather pale looking man in front of her.

'Thanks,' he mumbled, and returned quietly to his seat in the darkened cabin. Food had been served earlier and now most people had opted for sleep on this night flight from Johannesburg to Moscow via Amsterdam.

Settling himself down in his blue-striped seat, he pressed idly at some buttons on the armrest and put the seat back into a reclining position. He glanced across the aisle at the sleeping forms of Stuart and Len. They had all been very tired when the concert ended in South Africa and had eaten the dinner served on the plane almost automatically. Sam had not eaten any of the food that had been placed before him, but Benjamin had dug into it for him with gusto, and now lay with his huge frame sandwiched into the seat, making it appear even smaller than it was.

Trying to breathe calmly to steady his nerves, Sam began to play with the control buttons for the TV. He didn't feel well at all. In fact he felt quite ill. His hands were clammy and his teeth began to chatter. Reaching towards the discarded blanket on the floor, he pulled it up over himself and tried to snuggle into it.

Closing his eyes, he tried to blot out the rest of the world. It almost succeeded, but just as he was dozing off, Benjamin uttered a huge snort and Sam sat bolt upright. It was no good. Once more he undid his seatbelt and made his way toward the galley and the friendly stewardess.

Glancing up from the book that she was reading quietly in the corner, she took one admiring glance at his dark, stormy looks and sighed, wishing she had not just got engaged.

'What time do we land?' asked Sam, nervously running a hand over his unshaven face.

'Not for another five hours, I'm afraid,' she informed him quietly. Glancing at him more critically, she stood up straight and cleared her throat. 'This might be a shot in the dark, but would it help you to calm down if you saw the Captain? He can explain how things operate.'

Her soft, sultry tones were lost on him and he nodded quietly. 'Yeah.' He swallowed nervously. 'Yeah, that might not be such a bad idea.'

The stewardess nodded and indicated for Sam to follow her. She knocked before opening the cockpit door. After explaining the situation very briefly to the Captain, she gave Sam a warm smile and left quietly.

The Captain indicated a small spare seat behind him and Sam sat down. Calmly and quietly the Captain explained the radar equipment and the speed they were travelling at. When he asked if Sam had any questions, Sam nodded briefly at the whole array of lights in front of him.

'Yeah – I do have a question. Where would be the best place to sit if we were to – um – say, crash?'

The Captain answered as best he could, trying to put things as simply as possible without getting too technical. Finally Sam nodded, got up and left. Looking at his departing figure, the Captain felt slightly piqued that his narrative had been met with mere acknowledgement, and he turned to his co-pilot. 'Amazing that, isn't it?'

His co-pilot stretched and yawned, 'What?' He had paid little to no attention to Sam.

'Well, how can anyone not fall in love with flying? And fancy him asking to see my flying licence! Some cheek!'

His co-pilot reached for his Tic-Tacs and offered them to the Captain. 'Don't know really.' But he wasn't really interested in other people's fears and phobias. All he cared about was getting home safely to feed his dog. The Captain sat and oozed frustration quietly knowing that his co-pilot already had his mind on other things.

Stuart and Len were still fast asleep when Sam returned to his seat. Benjamin had woken during his absence and was now sitting across the aisle chatting up some foreign chick. The engines made a slight noise and once more Sam got up and went in search of the stewardess.

It was a very weary bunch that left the plane at Amsterdam. They were met by Adam, someone their manager had organised for them to make sure that their stop-over went smoothly. They followed the tall, slim figure as he escorted them down a separate passage, one which the other passengers were not privy to, and into a private lounge. Stuart was more or less of the same height as Adam, but that is where the similarities ended. Adam wore tight black jeans with a smart white shirt tucked tightly into them, and there was absolutely no mistaking the fact that he was gay, even if one was to discount his very feminine walk.

Adam stood tall and erect, showing them what the room had to offer with his over flowery hand gestures. His clean shaven jaw worked furiously as he spoke and his green eyes sparkled. Finally, he asked if there was anything any of them needed to make themselves more comfortable. 'If you want anything, please ring the bell.' He indicated to a small red button next to the phone, and continued very formally, 'Please make use of the bar fridge and I will fetch you just before we are due to take off. Thank you.' He almost seemed to bow his way out of the room, and Stuart marvelled at the fact that his jeans did not burst at the seams.

When the door was firmly closed behind them, they tossed their hand luggage into a corner and collapsed on the large couches. Their stay in Amsterdam would be short as it was just a plane transfer, so they did not require much in the form of refreshment. But the room provided some sanctuary from would-be autograph hunters.

True to his word, Adam returned to fetch them when the other passengers had already boarded the plane. They entered quietly and sat down almost unobserved in their first-class seats on the final leg of their flight.

It was a three-hour flight to Moscow and uneventful. In fact, it was one of the smoothest flights they had been on. On arrival, they descended from sunny skies down through snow-filled clouds onto the icy runway. The plane skidded slightly on landing and Sam grabbed the armrest of his chair frantically. But the plane came to an eventual and safe stop, much to his enormous relief.

This was to be the final stage of their world tour. It had, in fact, been quite a struggle to get permission to perform in Moscow. But their agent was good and now here they were.

They had not initially intended to perform here, but somehow their plans had changed.

Their first problem in Moscow came when they had tried to clear customs. The customs official, who smelt of coffee, had remained unbending in the face of four astounded band members and he made them unpack each and every piece of luggage. This in itself was a mission as there was so much. The actual equipment had, thankfully, gone ahead, or else they would have been there for ages. They had been promised faithfully by their manager that someone would be there to assist in their arrival arrangements, but this person had yet to appear.

Stuart had to give Benjy a nudge as he could see the rising temper in his face. 'Not worth it, man. We'll just be here for ages more.' Benjy nodded in reply and bit down hard on his tongue.

Finally they made their way out of customs and through the crowds of people who just seemed to be milling around without any purpose, towards a small man who held up a sign that read: STUART LOVE.

'You here for us, mate?' queried Benjy.

'Yes! I here for you. I take you to hotel.' The man was short, with a thick bushy beard, and he had a very heavy Russian accent. He seemed to be a bundle of fur as he was so well wrapped up against the cold and his face was barely showing under his fur hat.

'Thank goodness,' Benjy sighed. 'Get us out of here. It's like a madhouse.'

'Pardon?' The driver's English was not that good.

Benjy smiled and shook his head. 'Never mind, mate.' The driver nodded and with an unsmiling face helped them with their luggage and led the way to the waiting car. It was a rather weather beaten minibus with a trailer attached for their luggage.

Once all their stuff was loaded, they made their way out of

the airport and onto the road that would take them into Moscow. The journey seemed long and tiring and the endless potholes made even Stuart feel a bit nauseous. Sam had finally fallen asleep, thankful that he was once again on solid ground, his head resting on Len's shoulder. Len sat quietly gazing out of the frosted window, his thoughts miles away.

Benjy and Stuart exchanged a knowing look as they eyed the now calm and sleeping form of Sam.

There was a sigh of relief from all of them when they pulled up outside their hotel. The hotel was impressive, far grander than they expected, especially after having driven through parts of Moscow.

Once allocated their rooms, they all decided to retire for a good night's sleep. They were too tired to ponder much about the missing representative who should have been there to make their life a bit easier. They guessed he or she would put in an appearance sooner or later. No-one was actually paying much attention to them, so there wasn't much of a problem at the moment, but there could have been. And it was that small uncertainty that Stuart did not like too much.

'See you guys later,' Stuart said as he reached his floor. The others were too tired to do more than nod.

Finding his room, Stuart battled to open the door with his keycard. Just as he was about to give up and head back downstairs, it opened. 'Thank goodness!' he muttered to himself. Closing the door behind him with his shoulder, he tossed his case on the bed. The carpet was a rich deep green which complemented the cream curtains and the cream bedspread. The room was small, though, and the double bed took up most of the space. Most of his luggage occupied one corner of the room as it had been brought up earlier. All their heavy musical equipment was stored in a separate room adjoining Benjamin's room. The curtains were closed and the lights had come on automatically when he opened the door.

Noticing the small bar fridge in the corner, he grabbed a small bottle of Scotch. Then he pulled off his shoes and flung himself on the bed, absolutely exhausted. He reached across for the phone and put a call through to his manager in the UK.

Stephen answered cheerfully, as always. 'Stu! Great to hear from you! How are things going? Everything arranged?'

Stuart held the phone from his ear and looked at it in mild amusement. It was always difficult to get a word in edgeways with Stephen. He could hear him going on and on and finally he put the phone back to his ear. 'Stephen – Stephen! Wait a minute, man!'

Stephen paused. 'Sorry, Stu – what is it?' Stephen was quite a bit younger than the band members, but his enthusiasm had grabbed them from the start and they had decided to take a chance with him, even though he was not very experienced. And this was the first time that he had let them down. At the back of Stuart's mind was a small twinge of suspicion that he could not quite work out in his tired brain.

'Did you arrange for someone to meet us here at all? I mean, we were met by a driver from the hotel, but there didn't seem to be anyone else.' He waited tiredly for the answer, beginning to choke on his drink, which had gone down the wrong way.

'What do you mean? Of course I arranged a welcome party for you! What do you think I am? I would never leave my FAVOURITE band alone in a foreign country and to their own devices. Oh my God! What you must THINK of me!' Stephen exclaimed, and Stuart could visualise him waving his hands around, flustered, while he sat with his feet on his desk, leaning back on his chair with an ever present cigarette dangling gently from his red puffy lips.

Stuart was by now absolutely exhausted, and too tired to actually care what the answer would be. He tried to keep the rest of the conversation brief but it took a while to mollify Stephen. 'Listen, it is not too much of a problem at the moment as we have the contact details of our next few gigs, but it would have helped – know what I mean?' He cut Stephen short as he began to launch once more into exclamations and protests. 'Listen, I am really *really* tired right now, and all I want to do is sleep, so find out what you can and get back to me.'

He returned to consciousness slowly, at first barely aware of the frantic banging on the door. Turning towards the bedside clock, he knocked over the little empty bottles of scotch from the bar fridge that sat on the small wooden table next to his bed. He had fallen asleep with the bedside lamp on, fully clothed, except for his shoes 'Drat!' he swore. 'OK – OK,' he yelled, 'just a bloody minute – it's two o'clock in the bloody morning!' His brain felt as if it had been buried deep inside a pile of pink and yellow cotton wool. He flung back the bedclothes that had somehow managed to entwine his limbs in their evil web, and stumbled to the door in his crumpled clothes. Suddenly he was fully awake as he heard the desperate scratchings of a woman. 'Please, please let me in!' Normally he would not even have contemplated letting anyone in at this time of night, but there was something in her voice that put his usual caution on the back burner.

He moved quicker and yanked the door open. Taken unawares, it swung open violently. In front of him stood a young woman. She immediately pushed her way in and slammed the door behind her, then leant with her back pressed against it, he could see that her whole body was shaking, and her voice when she spoke filled the room with fear.

'I didn't think you would let me in.' She sounded

desperate. Catching her breath, she continued, this time accusingly, 'What took you so long?' This was obviously not a groupie; there seemed to be a distinct lack of 'groupism' in Moscow – not that he was complaining as it made a refreshing change. As for this young woman, she didn't even seem aware of who he was.

'A simple "thank you" would have been nice,' Stuart added almost to himself. The girl had already moved past him and was glancing anxiously out of the window.

He stumbled once more sleepily to the bed and lay down, curling himself up in the blankets. 'Care to tell me what's going on?' He yawned and stretched while watching her quietly. The whole situation seemed so bizarre, but he was too tired to think things through at this stage.

'No.' Nothing like a straight and simple answer. He yawned again and was about to ask another question when he saw her visibly stiffen. Listening, he could hear the sound of running footsteps coming down the corridor towards his room. Putting her finger to her lips, she glared at him to keep quiet. He did, more out of curiosity than anything else. He wondered, half idly, if he should be afraid, and that in itself made him curious.

There was knocking on the door next to his and the girl began to look around frantically. 'I must hide.' She looked at him. 'You hide me!' He sat on his bed surveying her. 'Quickly! Hide me.' There was more urgency and desperation to her voice.

She stood in front of him, vulnerable in her tight-fitting black pants and thick leather padded jacket. Her hair was covered with a dark woollen cap, but small tendrils of blonde hair escaped teasingly down the side of her face.

Unwinding himself from the bed, he stood facing her, unsure of what to do next. Grabbing his arms, she shook him slightly and whispered with a voice fraught with anxiety, 'They'll kill me! Can't you understand that?' She was getting more desperate, trying to make this man who stared at her like a guppy take the situation seriously, 'Please, for God's sake – you have to help me!' she pleaded.

It felt almost as if a switch went on inside him. He sprang to life and moved into action – and not a moment too soon. There was a knock on his door and a voice called out, 'Please open up. This is the police!'

He didn't respond for a minute, wanting them to think that he was asleep, and thus gaining a little time. They called out again, louder and more aggressively, 'Open up! This is the police!'

Stuart called from the bed, 'Coming!' Opening the door carefully, he peered out. 'Yes? What's going on?'

Two butch, fierce-looking policemen looked at him. Moisture had gathered in the folds of the tops of their jackets where the snow had fallen and then melted. There was no humour in their eyes, and although they spoke without menace, there was no mistaking the meaning behind their words.

'We're sorry to disturb you,' and as an afterthought, 'sir.' Stuart looked at them, and they continued, 'We believe that there is a very dangerous convict hiding somewhere on this floor. May we come in and have a look?' The last question was only a question in so much as that it was asked. The shorter of the two put his hand over the gun that hung carelessly by his pocket. Stuart was under no illusions that, should he fail to allow them access, they would force their way in anyway. He hadn't been here very long, but even to his inexperienced eyes he was beginning to doubt whether they actually were the police. But he had no intention of arguing against a loaded weapon.

He let them in. The bedside light was on and the bedding on the bed had been hastily thrown to one side as he got up. The policemen gave the room a cursory glance and opened the cupboards and looked in the bathroom. Opening the small french window that led onto the rickety balcony, they looked out.

They shut the window again and the room was suddenly freezing from the blast of cold air that had been let in. 'Thank you. We will not disturb you again tonight.' As they walked towards the door, one of them stopped abruptly and pausing with his hand on the doorknob looked back at Stuart with a piercing almost questioningly look. Stuart returned the look, not daring to breathe, and then, suddenly, they opened the door and left, closing it with a final click.

There followed a few minutes of absolute silence while Stuart held his breath. He could hear them make their way further down the corridor as he switched off the bedside lamp and opened the curtains to let the light in from the street lamp. Carefully he lifted the bundle of blankets and sheets from the other side of the bed. The young girl raised her head and her black knitted cap fell from her head revealing long blonde hair.

He was about to ask a question, but she forestalled him by putting her fingers against his lips. She leant forward and whispered in his ear, 'Not now. Later. I want to make sure that they are gone first.'

Nodding, he leant back against the headboard of the bed and listened to the fading noises in the corridor. He felt his heart pounding in his chest. The girl lay next to him and he was suddenly very aware of his unkempt state. He got up, pondering the thought that all of this was so unlike him. It was obviously the sheer exhaustion of the last few days that was responsible. He walked to the window and peered out at the dark night. From his window he could see the Kremlin and St Basil's Cathedral, both lit up around Red Square, where Lenin lay on display. It seemed almost justified that Lenin's last wish to be buried with his wife would remain unfulfilled, but then he wasn't here to judge. Every country had a past, some more glorified than others.

Climbing back onto the bed, he lay and listened. In the distance he finally heard the sound of sirens disappearing into the quietness of the night. Stuart turned questioningly to the girl and found her asleep. Typical, he thought. Here he was lying awake and the reason for his wakefulness at this time in the morning was fast asleep!

He watched for a while as she breathed in and out, in and out, and finally decided against prodding her awake. He couldn't sleep now as his mind was racing, so he got up and paced in the small space allowed between the bed, window and dressing table. What the hell was going on here? he wondered to himself, and uttered these thoughts out loud to the girl as he heard her utter a soft moan.

As she turned slightly and looked at him, he could see a small amount of blood slowly oozing out of her, making a deep red circle on his white rumpled sheets. He touched her gently and found her to be ice-cold. Oh no! Here she was, dying on him! This situation could not get worse – or so he thought.

Panicking, he grabbed for the phone, remembering just in time that it was a very foolish thing to do under the circumstances. What would he say? How would he explain that the suddenly missing girl was actually here in his room after all, and that she needed urgent medical attention? How could he explain the wound? Their suspicions would focus on him, and who could blame them. God! What a horrible rotten mess he had got himself into!

Going into the bathroom, he fetched a towel and gently lifted her top to find a small stab wound just below her ribs. He dabbed at it and then, fetching a shirt of his, tore it and used part as a pad and the rest to bandage it tightly. As he lowered her shirt, she moaned softly again.

'Ssh,' he said, 'it's going to be OK.'

She opened one eye. 'Yes I know.' And indicating the wound she continued, 'It was only skin deep, there was no need to panic.'

‘I was not, thank you very much.’ He was irritated that she could dismiss his workmanship so lightly.

She snorted a small sound and turned her head and went back to sleep. He could not believe this! She was not in the least bit thankful for what he had done and she should be. After all, didn’t he just save her life? Not once, but twice! Women! He sat there and watched her sleep, his questions for the moment going unanswered.

10

Nikolai threw a small clear plastic bag onto the untidy, work-laden desk. It lay there like an object out of place and beckoned to Robert to open it, but still he hesitated – uncertain. He rubbed a hand across his unshaven face and stared mesmerised at it. A stray ray of sunshine caught hold of something in the packet and, as if to throw out a challenge, revealed a fleeting image of a multi-coloured rainbow across the far wall. Its red tentacles beckoned to him as if to say, 'Touch me – go on – touch me if you dare!' He shivered as images of his recent nightmare passed over him.

Nikolai watched Robert, noticing the sudden involuntary shiver, and for a few seconds said nothing. Robert reached a big strong hand over to the bag and, opening it, tossed the contents mercilessly out onto the dusty desk top. There in the weak sunlight lay a key, a watch and an old stub from a plane ticket. He looked at Nikolai. 'Is this all that you could find?'

'Yes, strange about that, isn't it?' He leant back in his chair. 'It's almost as if someone knew about the old man before we did…' His sentence was left unfinished and he looked enquiringly at Robert. Had Robert known about him? Had MI6 been doing their own investigations?

Robert idly turned the key around in his hand, ignoring the hidden connotation in Nikolai's voice. 'How did you know that he was connected with Patrick?'

Nikolai explained that the body of an old man had been fished out of the river, and purely by chance one of the policemen on duty had recognised him and alerted his superiors. Nikolai avoided an in-depth discussion of how and where the policeman had known the old man. But it was when the information had filtered up the system that alarm bells started to ring in certain areas; namely the FSB. They had acted as quickly as they could once they had received the information, but not quickly enough. By the time they had got to the apartment it had been cleaned thoroughly. But someone had missed the small trap door in the floor under the bed.

'Aah! The proverbial trap door.' Robert smiled inwardly. It was almost the same as keeping your money under the mattress instead of in a bank.

'Yes. Good for us that it was missed, otherwise we wouldn't have these vital pieces of information,' Nikolai continued, almost a little too casually. 'What do you think?' He eyed Robert keenly.

'I'm still not too sure how you can be certain that he was connected with Patrick.' He raised questioning eyes to Nikolai.

Nikolai scratched his chin and leant back in his chair. 'We saw them together.' He stopped and tapped his finger quietly on the desk. He didn't look up at Robert and Robert knew that he was weighing up how much information to volunteer. Finally he sighed. 'Patrick's involvement with us was – well, let's just say–' He stopped, wondering how to proceed further. 'Well – it was restricted to certain areas, if I could put it that way, and about ten years ago, both he and the old man helped us out in a little operation in Africa. And before you ask,' as he could see Robert raising his eyes questioningly, 'the information is top-secret and I myself haven't even seen it.' When Nikolai had first started making enquiries about Patrick and the old man, some doors began to close in his face. This in itself had irked him, but that apart, it had been a cause of concern for him that was plaguing him and keeping him awake at night. What did those files contain? What was on them that he wasn't to know? Who was this man Patrick? They didn't know all that much about him, except what they were able to glean from the information that they had access to. He passed a rather dilapidated-looking folder over to Robert. There was no harm in him reading it as it didn't contain anything of a sensitive nature.

Taking the file, Robert opened it and read the one brief page that had been typed out. He assumed, incorrectly, that it was Nikolai who had removed any additional information that had been in the file.

He learnt that Patrick was the only son to an Irish mother and Russian father, both killed when he was in his late teens in a car accident. He had been devoted to his only surviving family – an uncle and aunt – and had at one time taken a girl there by the name of Natasha, having rescued her from a rather run-down orphanage just outside Minsk.

Further information about how he got his finances and his businesses was scant, but Nikolai told him he had a sneaking suspicion, that as yet remained unconfirmed, that Patrick had worked for more than one person or organisation.

Robert nodded and accepted the fact that Nikolai had opted for caution and that he would not be told any more specifics at this point. He knew not to ask, 'What little operation?', although he felt that this bit of missed information could prove vital further down the line. But for now he was prepared to let Nikolai get his own way.

Picking up his mug of lukewarm coffee, he idly traced the hairline crack with his forefinger. Raising the cup to his lips he took a sip, grimacing inwardly at the horrendous taste it offered. He looked across at Nikolai. 'Do you realise that this could mean more than we have up till now suspected?'

Nikolai nodded. 'Yes, my friend. I suggest that we start to

tread very carefully from now on. There is something going on here that even I don't know about, and I think that you feel the same?'

'We need to find out where this key fits in.' Robert picked it up and had a closer look. 'It's definitely a safe-deposit key – let me have a look at that ticket stub.' Nikolai obligingly passed it over and Robert frowned as he looked at it. 'This was for a flight to Heathrow a couple of months ago.' He thought for a minute, 'I wonder if this key could fit one of the safe deposit boxes there.'

'I suppose it is worth a try. I'll get someone onto it.'

'No, I'll do it.' Robert paused. 'That is, if you trust me?'

Nikolai glanced at his friend. The subject of trust had been raised once more, and he frowned to himself.

Robert continued, 'I have to go back to London anyway for a few days.'

Nikolai nodded and added with a smile, 'Sure – no problem.' He picked up the phone and ordered his secretary to book a flight for Robert to the UK. Ten minutes later the phone rang and the flight was confirmed.

Robert rose and shook hands with Nikolai. 'Be very careful, my friend. We appear to be gathering enemies. And I don't think I can protect you,' Nikolai told him, and Robert, with a serious and contemplative look, left the building.

Climbing into the back of the waiting car, he sighed a small sigh of relief. It would be good to get back to the UK, even if it was only for a day or two. He felt a small shiver of anxiety as he passed the Kremlin. The problem seemed to be gaining momentum and he didn't know quite how to proceed or from which angle to begin to tackle the problem. He sensed Nikolai's hidden fear and realised with a shock that he had every right to be afraid. He couldn't understand the extent of the damage that had been incurred, but he had a feeling that it was more complicated than he had at first thought.

Weariness began to creep up on him and the snowy

scenery around him began to blend into one blank white canvas, occasionally speckled with a smidgen of grey, almost as if someone had made a mistake when putting ink to paper and had taken a wet thumb to it to try and get rid of their error. He shifted in his seat as his eyes began to grow heavy and his mind began to wander peacefully. Strange, he thought to himself in one brief, clear moment, he didn't normally feel sleepy in a car and it was not as if he was tired. In fact, when he had left Nikolai his brain had been racing with a thousand unanswered questions, but now, it was almost as if he was so tired he didn't care.

Slowly he became aware of a queasy feeling in the pit of his stomach, and somewhere in his mind he thought that it would be wise to make a stop. Slowly and surprisingly painfully he pulled up his weary, sick body and knocked on the glass partition that separated him from the driver. The driver took no notice. Now Robert realised that he was in trouble and desperately tried to open his heavy eyelids. In slow motion he scrambled towards the door handles and in a daze discovered they were locked. As if in some horror movie where one could not move for fear, he lethargically began to bang more intensely on the partition, but the driver kept on ignoring him. He even began to doubt that he was banging on the partition. Maybe he hadn't even moved and that was why the driver hadn't stopped. It felt just like a horrible nightmare from which he could never escape.

The weariness was creeping into his very bones and finally the struggle to escape just felt unreachable and he slumped onto the floor. Something had been put into the back of the car, and whatever it was, was working like a dream. And on that note he blacked out, just as a flash of red penetrated his consciousness.

The car began to pick up speed and carried its silent passenger towards it's ultimate destination.

* * *

Hours or maybe days later he awoke and found himself sitting on a wooden chair. He didn't know where he was and had no idea of how long he had been like this. His legs were tied with a rope, as were his arms, which had been tied behind his back. He felt awful. His head hurt, his mouth tasted of sawdust and his limbs felt weary and heavy.

Trying to feel his fingers, he soon realised that the bonds were so tight that the circulation to his hands had practically ceased. He tried to wriggle his fingers once more, but it proved fruitless. Was that his little finger he could feel? 'Aaagghh,' he moaned quietly to himself. He doubted that he could possibly have felt worse. In fact it was like a very bad case of flu.

His neck felt stiff and he wondered how long he'd been asleep. There was a blindfold over his eyes, and the tightness of it made the back of his eyeballs burn. He heard a small cough and soon the sharp, unmistakable smell of a cigar filled the air. It made him feel ill and he leant forward, retched horribly a few times and threw up. Mercifully he passed out again.

11

It was late morning when there was a slight tap on the door. 'You awake yet, Stu?' Benjy's voice sounded slightly muffled through the wooden panels.

'Just a minute.' Stuart walked towards the door and opened it carefully. Peering down the corridor he looked at Benjy. 'You alone, mate?'

'Yeah, the others went to see the Kremlin.' He yawned and stretched. 'I didn't feel like going and wondered what you were up to.' Suddenly he seemed to focus in on the other's face. 'Hey, what's up? You look kinda weird.' And as if a thought suddenly entered his normally carefree mind, 'You didn't want to go, did you, mate? I mean, you don't feel left out or anything? We did try to phone you but it was engaged, so we figured you had taken it off the hook. Damn good thing too if you ask me.' He added in a rather pretentious tone, 'One needs one's beauty sleep, after all, doesn't one?' Benjy had the ability to wrap you up in a blanket of 'Benjyness' that made one feel all warm and toasty.

'No, it's not that. I'm just a bit jet-lagged still – you know how it gets.' Stuart looked down at the carpet, avoiding the drummer's astute gaze.

'Yeah, I know, mate.' suddenly Benjy became aware of the fact that he was still standing in the corridor. 'Well, are you going to let me in or what? Can't stand in the corridor all morning, you know.'

'Sorry, Benj.' He moved aside for Benjy to enter, but stopped him when he had one foot in the room and put his finger to his lips. Leaning forward he whispered in his ear, 'Don't say anything. Not one word, OK?'

He had no idea what Stuart was on about but intrigued, agreed nevertheless. He was a very easy-going bloke and nothing much bothered him. As he walked further into the room he heard the shower and looked questioningly at his friend. His look was returned with a small smile. What exactly was his friend up to? He hoped that he hadn't just hopped into bed with the first stranger he met, because it was not what Stuart was about. He was not a bed-hopper and, besides, when had he possibly had time to meet someone? Half of Benjy felt extremely impressed that his friend had managed to find someone so quickly, but the other half oozed unease.

Stuart turned the TV on. It would, in some way, diminish the sound of their voices, or at the very least confuse their dialogue, should anyone be listening in. And he did not particularly want Elizabeth to know that he had company.

'You sly old dog, you!' whispered Benjy with a knowing but questioning smile all over his face. His smile froze, however, as he looked at Stuart, and the small knot of concern that he felt tightened just a bit.

Stuart did not return the smile, nor did he look like a cat who had swallowed the cream. In fact, he looked stressed out, and the otherwise unobservant Benjy suddenly became aware. 'Are you in some kind of trouble?'

Stuart nodded. 'I think so. She's a real bitch, you know.' He flung himself down on his bed. 'She shows no appreciation for what I've done for her. None!'

He paused as if to gather his thoughts. Benjamin battled to keep from laughing out loud. Suddenly he felt better about the situation. Perching himself next to Stuart on the bed, he leant closer to hear what Stuart was saying.

Stuart told him the whole story, albeit briefly as he himself didn't know too much at this stage. 'I need to ask you a favour. Can you somehow find a chemist or some shop around here and buy some hair colour?'

His friend nodded and with a puzzled look gazed almost unseeingly at the bathroom door. 'Sure, I'll do you the favour, but Stuart.' He paused and frowned. 'I'm not too sure about this whole thing.' Stuart stared at the floor, listening to his friend's voice as it continued, 'Do you actually know what you are getting yourself into? I mean, this could be serious stuff.' Stuart picked up the cautious note in the otherwise easy-going Benjy's voice.

They were quiet for a few minutes, then Stuart cleared his throat. Scratching his head, he turned to face Benjy. 'I know, mate, I know. It all seems a little odd.' He paused and clenched his hands tightly together. 'She needs my help. And I just feel in some strange way that I can't let her down.'

He didn't have to add that he had been thinking of Anne and how he was unable to protect her. That was written all over his face, and Benjy understood. He actually understood more about Stuart than the other members of the band. Putting a casual hand on his leg, he nodded. 'It's OK…' He left the rest of his sentence unfinished. 'I won't be long.' He stood up and went out of the room. Closing the door quietly behind him, his hand remained on the handle for a few seconds as his mind worked overtime. Finally he shook his head as if to clear his random thoughts. He had not missed the noticeable spark in his friend's eyes.

Passing the cleaning lady, he gave her one of his warm, friendly smiles. She in turn looked at him as if he had crawled out of the cheese. Oh well, he shrugged, you win some – you lose some.

He returned to his room to fetch his coat, gloves and scarf before he made his way out of the hotel. The cold air hit him with a force and he coughed as it tickled the back of his throat. 'Hope I'm not in for a cold,' he muttered to himself. He was always a bit over-cautious about his health. He walked straight back into the hotel, past the doorman and in through the rotating glass door, the reception area was quiet and he had no problem in attracting the attention of the receptionist. 'Excuse me, do you speak English?'

The girl was young and beautiful. With sad, haunted eyes she walked towards him. 'Yes – leetle.' Her voice had the heavy accent of all local Muscovites. Her blonde hair streamed out behind her in a sheet of pure gold and silver. It was unfortunate that she had opted to cover her face in a garish amount of make-up, as she would have been far more beautiful and perfect without it.

Nearly forgetting himself, Benjamin put on his most charming smile and coughed slightly. Indicating his chest, he queried, 'I think I'm getting a cold. Is there a chemist anywhere near here?'

'Keemist?' she asked raising her etched eyebrows ever so slightly.

'Yeah! Keemist. But I need to let you in on a little secret as well.' He indicated to her to lean closer to him. 'My hair – it needs colour – you understand?'

A small secretive smile coated her blood-red lips and she nodded. 'Yees, kolor.' She understood only too well as she flung back her own hair. She then proceeded to indicate the direction which he should take.

As he turned round to walk back through the door and out into the cold, she looked towards a man sitting reading a paper and shook her head. He acknowledged this and carried on reading.

It took Benjamin far longer to find the shop than he would have liked. But once there, he made his purchase and walked casually back into the hotel, giving a broad smile and a wink as he passed the receptionist.

In his own mind he was plotting how he could get her to himself and bury himself in that gorgeous hair of hers. Yes, he thought to himself when she returned his warm smile, there was a definite possibility of further developing British/Russian relations here. And he was all for improvement.

12

Nikolai had spent the better part of the last few days trying to identify the girl who had died with Patrick, but he was still none the wiser. They had used what little bits of teeth they could find to try and establish an identity through dental records, but that had proved fruitless. They had approached virtually every dentist known to them, but still nothing. A small bit of the label of one of her dresses had survived, and they had explored this avenue, but without a face they could not go very far. He began to fear that the woman would forever remain nameless, and somehow this bothered him. He did not want to think that there was no one out there who cared whether this woman lived or died, but with each passing day, he very much began to fear that this was the case. It would only be much later on in their investigation that they would be able to put a name to this innocent victim. A woman, totally unrelated to their investigation. Someone who had been so hungry for food, that she had been scratching through the bins in the car park.

Leaning back in his chair, he glanced out of the window. It was warmer today but it was snowing again. He sighed and picked up the phone once more. 'Get me London.' It had been a week since he had heard from Robert.

The ring of the phone echoed in the silent office. Nikolai picked it up. 'Hello.' There was a pause as he waited. 'Yes, can I please speak to Robert Brown?' There was another delay which seemed to drag on. He idly started to flick at his pen and wondered why it was taking so long. The snow still drifted softly past his window and as he watched, it started to gather momentum. Soon, thousands of snow flakes fell past his window, all in a rush to establish their place, albeit for a short time, on earth. Then their exquisite and unique beauty melted into little puddles.

He was about to give up and dial again when he heard a crackling on the other end of the line and a small voice spoke. 'I'm sorry, sir, but' – there was hesitation on the other side, almost as if he was listening to someone else and taking advice from them before he continued – 'I'm sorry sir,' he repeated, 'but we have not heard from him for quite some time.' The voice grew silent on the other end, as did the crackling on the phone. It seemed for a moment as if everyone was holding their breath.

Nikolai swallowed the small lump in his throat and slowly raised himself into an upright position. 'What?' he croaked, and almost choked on his fear. 'You have not heard from him?' His brain began to work in illogical circles. 'But that is not possible,' he stammered, more to himself than the unknown identity on the other end of the phone.

The voice on the phone listened quietly and then crackled back to life and asked him to hold.

'Yes – I'll hold.' He began to shake. A small, nervous tremor edged its way into his hands. Breathe! Slowly – calmly – just breathe, for Pete's sake! Keep calm. He had to keep calm!

Soon a cultured voice came over the phone and the crackling that had been so apparent during his earlier conversation was missing, 'Is that Nikolai Sebislav?'

'Yes.' There seemed no point in denying it at this stage. 'And to whom am I speaking?' He prided himself on the fact that his voice betrayed none of the physical attributes of nervousness that were now very obvious to him with the shaking of his hands and the cold clammy dampness of his forehead.

'I'm Malcolm Pool, chief of defence staff of the Prime Minister's military advisors.' He paused, and Nikolai swallowed hard. 'We have been looking for Robert for a week now. Can you tell us where he is?' Malcolm sat quite comfortably in a luxurious leather chair across the desk from the British Prime Minister who was leaning forward, listening intently to Malcolm's side of the conversation. His top lip was etched in slight perspiration as he waited with baited breath, his thin hands tightly clasped in front of him. Of medium build, he was neat and tidy, with his short, grey curly hair carefully parted and combed. On his nose sat a pair of reading glasses that he never wore in public as his pride would not allow it. He looked across at Malcolm with small, beady, selfish eyes, wishing he could hear the other side of the conversation.

In one well-manicured hand Malcolm carefully held a very clever forgery of a telegram which was clear and to the point:

> CLASSIFICATION: TOP SECRET: XOSMIC
> REF TEL: 097
>
> SUBJECT CONFIRMED DEFECTED. CONTACTS MADE. GRATEFUL ADVICE OPERATION PHOENIX
>
> COOLE

The telegram ended, as diplomatic protocal dictated with the name of the Ambassador to Russia and was a very good forgery, even if Malcolm had to admit it himself. He had no idea from where it had come, but it suited him no end to have their slightly troubling situation at an end. And if either he or the PM was ever questioned about it, they could use the age-old excuse of plausible deniability.

Nikolai sat quietly at his desk as the implication of the new information he had received began to register, and he was slowly beginning to smell a rat. He had not been in this business for as long as he had without being able to tell if something was not quite right. And this was not quite right. But what was wrong here? He had to clear his mind – to think. He couldn't quite work it out, but of one thing he was sure, and that was that Robert Brown had not defected.

If this was how the game was being played, then he realised without a doubt that his life was in danger; and if Robert was missing then he was in even more danger than he initially suspected. But where was it coming from? Who was behind it all? What little he already knew, coupled together with this latest information, did anything but create a clear picture.

Baffled, he spoke quietly on the phone and the conversation ended shortly, with both sides agreeing to phone should they hear from Robert.

Nikolai slammed down the phone and frowned. He would have to think. And think fast.

The well-manicured hand of Malcolm Pool replaced the receiver. Looking with a satisfied smile at the Prime Minister, he said, 'It's like killing two birds with one stone. Most satisfactory result, PM.'

Don Brett, who had worked with, trained and been a good friend to Robert Brown, had just asked for an interview with Malcolm Pool and was being ushered in. As head of MI6, he was used to getting the information he wanted and needed. He was neither intimidated nor afraid of confrontation. He was highly respected within his organisation and with those he came into contact with. He was an honourable man, and one always knew where one stood with him.

He was also tall and strong, with noticeable grey streaks in his short dark wavy hair. His navy pinstriped suit looked good on him, as did most things. He knew it too, and took great pride in looking good. He *enjoyed* looking good.

Malcolm stood up and greeted him with a handshake. 'Good to see you, Don. Please take a seat.' He indicated the dark blue leather chairs opposite his desk, then made his way across the plush plum-coloured carpet to the liquor cabinet and pulled out a bottle of Chivas. With his back to Don he asked, 'Would you like a drink?'

Don noticed the evasive posture, however insignificant it may have seemed. He was a good agent and could tell when even the slightest thing was out of place. This annoyed his sixteen-year-old daughter very much! He shook his head in the negative. A drink might cloud his mind and he wanted to be as sharp as he could be under the circumstances.

He watched as Malcolm retreated back behind his desk with tumbler in hand. Everything about the advisor was neat and there was not much out of place. From the top of his thin, fair little head through his neat dark blue suit down to his over-polished black shoes, Don disliked him. He couldn't put his finger on exactly what it was that he disliked about him, but he just did.

'What can I do for you?' Malcolm casually lifted his glass to his lips and took a sip.

As Don watched him swallow the amber liquid, he asked the question that Malcolm knew he would ask. 'I hear that you received a telegram about one of my agents.'

Slowly Malcolm replaced the glass on the desk in front of him, careful to manoeuvre a coaster underneath it, and licked his lips in a slow and deliberate manner. Pressing his hands together, he raised them casually to his mouth and coughed very slightly. He eyed Don slyly, and deciding that it was perhaps best not to beat about the bush, he answered, 'Yes.'

'Can I see that telegram please?' He held out his hand and Malcolm slowly lifted his glass and took a deliberate sip, before teasingly replacing the drink back on the desk. His voice was a little gruff when he replied, 'I'm afraid I don't have it.'

Don's voice became deathly quiet, 'I learn that you have received a telegram that states that one of my *best* agents has defected.' He paused in order to try and squash his absolute fury. 'And then you deny me access to that telegram. Do you expect me to accept this without a word of doubt?' Don was furious. In fact he was beyond furious.

Malcolm put his elbows on the table and leant across the desk towards Don. He smiled a cold and heartless smile. 'Yes.' The stench of whisky on his breath hit Don's nostrils like a damp face-cloth and he recoiled in disgust.

'I see.' Don got up and walked straight out of the office without a backwards glance. He was not going to give Malcolm the satisfaction of knowing his next step.

Malcolm, irritated, banged his fists down on the desk. Drat that man! Who does he think he is anyway? he thought. Malcolm's cool, calm composure left him and he stormed furiously over to the drinks cabinet to pour himself another stiff drink. Tossing it back in one swift movement, he slammed the empty glass down on the counter so hard it shattered. Tiny bits of glass cut into his hand, but he was too angry to notice or care.

Don, in his turn, returned to his office, slamming the door on his way in. He threw himself, frustrated, into his big black leather chair. Leaning his head back, he stared at the ceiling. He'd be damned if he was going to let that smooth-talking aristocratic arse ride roughshod over him. Suddenly he flew out of his chair, all action. He knew exactly what he was going to do. It took him barely two hours to disappear successfully, and ten hours later a gangly teenager entered Moscow.

Later that afternoon, Malcolm received a call, 'What do you mean he's gone?' He listened to the voice on the other end. 'I don't give a fuck! You waited too long – now find him!' He slammed the phone down and wrenched the tie from around his neck, flinging it viciously across the room. His hand had now stopped bleeding and he reached for the bottle of Chivas. Not bothering with a glass this time, he undid the top and took a deep, long swig.

13

The freshness of the breeze brought with it a tinge of ice, something which seemed to be lost on Elizabeth as she wandered out of the hotel with Stuart's arm draped casually around her shoulders. Neither the receptionist nor the man reading the paper in the corner recognised this short-haired girl. The girl they were looking for had long blonde hair and this girl had a deep shade of auburn. They gave them a casual glance, and then lost interest in them altogether; a decision which they would live to regret and one that they would be made to pay for.

Elizabeth and Stuart walked like that for about ten minutes, glancing occasionally behind them to make sure that they were not being followed. Finally, sure that there was no one behind them, she released a pent up breath of air and leant against the small, dirty stone wall that protected the Moskva River from the rest of the world. Part of it was covered in snow.

Her breathing was heavier than normal. Stuart looked at her face and noticed the effort with which she was concentrating. He touched her arm. 'Hey, are you all right?'

She was finding it hard enough to breathe in the cold, let alone with a wound, but she nodded. 'Yeah – no problems.' She turned to face him, and her face softened for a second. 'Thank you.'

He was slightly taken aback at this and looked at her with some concern. 'Are you sure that you're OK?'

She laughed at him. 'Of course I'm OK.'

'But last night...' He left his sentence unfinished

'Yes, last night was a bit of a problem, wasn't it?' She looked at him angrily for a split second. 'But it is my problem and not yours!' Seeing his friendly face close up, she realised that she sounded a little bit ungrateful, but she didn't want him involved in this mess. Didn't want him caught up in a potentially fatal and explosive situation. 'I'm sorry, I don't mean to be so rude, but you really can't concern yourself with this.' She paused and looked deep into his eyes. 'It's dangerous, Stuart.' Reaching out, she put one small gloved hand on his arm as if to reassure him that all would be OK. 'Trust me, you do not want to get involved in this.'

'But–'

She cut him short. 'There are no buts. I told you that this is my problem and not yours, so leave it alone and forget you ever saw me.' Her voice softened again. 'Please?'

He looked at her, feeling slightly hurt but mollified by the soft tone in her voice. It seemed like hours, but in reality was only a few minutes that they stood there, facing each other, each one trying to come to their own conclusion. Finally he broke the silence. 'OK – if that's what you want,' he agreed, and even to his own ears he sounded a little bit sulky, which surprised him as it was not like him at all.

'Yes, Stuart – please, leave well alone.' She silently removed her hand from his arm and kissed him lightly on his cold cheek. Turning around she walked off and he stood there, feeling helpless as he watched her go.

Suddenly he ran after her. 'Wait!'

He had no idea why he did that, but she stopped and turned to face him. 'Yes?'

'I just wanted to say that if you ever needed me at any time – any time at all.' He paused. 'Please call me – I will come, be it day or night. Just call – please.' He was suddenly eager for her to know that he cared. What was wrong with him? What was it about this woman that made him act like a stupid teenager?

'Thanks, but no, I won't need you again.' She felt almost sorry for him as she watched a small flicker of something unreadable cross his face.

He reached out to her gloved hands and placed in them an untidy piece of paper with his name and number hastily scrawled over it. 'I hear what you are saying, but please, if you ever change your mind – phone me.' He was suddenly very afraid for her and didn't want to let her go.

'Thank you.' She pulled her hands gently from his, wondering briefly whether, if they had met at a different time, things might have been different. She sighed softly to herself, and once more turned to go. This time she would not stop, and he would not run after her.

He watched as she grew smaller and smaller. A small black figure against a backdrop of white snow. Eventually she disappeared out of sight. Finally he turned, and as he did so he saw the sunlight filter through the clouds and touch the walls of the Kremlin. He shivered, and with his hands buried deep into his pockets he walked back towards the hotel, and on the way back threw the empty bottle of hair dye into a waste paper basket.

Unlike Stuart, who had the girl on his mind, Elizabeth Curll didn't give Stuart another thought as she walked away from him. Her mind was going over the events of last night and it all seemed a bit of a mess. She walked over to St Basil's and bought a ticket to go in, then wandered around aimlessly until she found a small corner with a bench in it which was slightly hidden from view.

Sitting there, she watched the tourists wander past, feeling slightly amused at their facial expressions as they admired the ancient stone building. Many of them tried to throw arms out of the tiny windows to wave to their friends below. One of the many things stupid tourists did on holiday. She shrugged to herself, supposing that it could be worse. Soon her thoughts turned away from tourists to the real problem that she was facing. She wished that she hadn't been so hasty. But she had always been like that, just going where the fancy took her – and in this case, where a faint whiff of something afoot took her.

She sat there quietly for about ten minutes and then a man joined her.

'What happened to you last night?' He looked ahead of him then turned to face her. 'I could have done without waiting around for you for well over an hour!' He was angry and she couldn't really blame him.

'I'm sorry, but I couldn't help it.' She looked him directly in the eyes. 'I was having a look at something that I perhaps shouldn't have, and I was caught.' She finished the last bit of her sentence almost apologetically, knowing she had risked blowing the whole operation.

'What?' She had his full attention now, as well as his fury. 'How did you get away?' he mumbled through clenched teeth while his fingers played curiously with his dirty-pink entrance ticket.

'I was lucky.' She paused, and finished softly, ' And I met someone who helped me.'

'Does he know who you are?' he questioned her, almost wishing he could throttle her and her chance taking! He knew only too well that sooner or later her luck would run out, and he rather figured it would be sooner. Drat the girl! 'It's very important that this mission is not jeopardised until we find the main man.' His angry words fell like little daggers around her, and she realised that he was justified in being angry with her.

She smiled wryly. 'No, all he knows is that my name is Elizabeth. He probably enjoyed a bit of excitement in his life for a change.'

'Do you know who he was?' he continued harshly, not giving an inch.

She nodded. 'Yes, Stuart someone or other.'

His hand stopped what it was doing. 'Stuart? Please don't tell me it was Stuart Love?' He knew that the band was in town, and the irony of Stuart being mixed up in this, albeit in a small almost insignificant role, amused him a great deal.

She looked at him curiously. 'Yes, actually I think it was now that you mention it, but it really isn't important.'

'It just might be.' He laughed silently to himself, relaxing suddenly. Fancy Stuart getting caught up with all of this. 'Anyway, down to business. What do you know so far?'

'Well, it seems really odd but Robert Brown has disappeared and there seems to be no trace of him at the moment,' she continued in her soft voice, not at all wounded at his aggression and annoyance. 'Also Don Brett has left London and we can only assume that he is here in Moscow about now. But it looks as if the Intelligence Service have lost track of him completely.'

The man nodded. 'I agree with you about Robert Brown. Maybe we were wrong in our initial assumption. What do you think?'

They remained discussing various new details and angles with their heads bent close together. Time dragged on and finally they left as they had come, separately.

14

It was the slap of ice-cold water that brought Robert Brown shrieking back to consciousness – a single act which dramatically reminded him of his captive state. Instinctively he knew that his life depended on staying alert. Slowly he mulled the thought around in his head that he had to be valuable to his captors or else they would have killed him already.

An isolated drop of ice-cold water followed a silent rugged path down his now unshaven face. There was no way that he could see anything at the moment. The black sack tied around his head made sure of that. But his other senses were working. The air was thick with the cloying smell of vomit – his. The sweet smell of cigar tobacco assaulted his nostrils and there was another strong smell, as yet unidentifiable. He tilted his head to one side, silently trying to work out what it was.

Two sets of manipulative hands grabbed him firmly by the tops of his arms and dumped him onto a chair. Struggling was useless as his arms remained firmly tied behind him, and besides he simply did not have the energy at the moment.

Robert listened intently to his surroundings. Someone cleared their throat and he picked up on it immediately. Working things out silently in his mind, he figured that there were at least four of them in the room besides himself: the goons who had grabbed him, Mr Phlegmy and the man who had not moved or spoken since Robert was brought into the room. But he was there all right, kneeling or sitting very close to him – so close that he could almost feel the touch of his breath on his face.

Of course, it was possible that there were others, but for now he would rely on the information he had picked up. It was important that he remain alert and constantly update himself on his surroundings before sleep deprivation and interrogation techniques began to take their toll.

The fact that he was alive and not worm food comforted him. His captors would not be taking these steps or wasting their time if it was a simple execution. Neither did Robert think he would be held to ransom. If that was their intention, then they would be pretty disappointed as the British Government's policy ruled out all possibility of paying ransoms. So the only other obvious option was that they wanted information. And he wondered what that information was.

It would be easy to panic in this situation, but if he was going to survive he had to remember his training. First step – remain calm, second step – recognise the interrogation techniques and remember how to counter them. Every operative underwent extensive training by the SAS in surviving interrogations and what to expect. But unless you stayed calm and thought, you might as well not have bothered.

Robert stayed absolutely still and tried to concentrate. Nobody had as yet spoken, but when they did, he was hoping to pick up on the languages and accents used. As if on cue, a strong hand raised his head and a long stream of cigar smoke blew into his face and filtered up his nostril and down his throat making him cough hoarsely. 'Tired?' The voice was rough and guttural. Robert did not reply and remained still. He guessed that the accent was Eastern European, probably Russian, and that comforted him. He was a Russian speaker himself and that would be a great advantage, unless of course they knew that. He wondered how much they actually did know about him.

The door opened and a blast of icy air once more encompassed the room. The door closed again and the refreshing moment of freedom was snuffed out. He had not heard any footsteps from the men who were already in the room with him, so it was reasonable to assume that at least one more person had entered and none had left. He strained his ears to discern the slightest sound, but this task was almost impossible as the wind had picked up outside, hurling and screaming in a high-pitched, whiny voice against the windows and door. The more he strained his ears to listen, the more the wind seemed to tease him. An overwhelming wave of dizziness gripped him and he nearly passed out. The feeling went away and he tried to concentrate on regaining his composure. Whatever they had given him to knock him out had been pretty effective.

Once again the door opened and the sharp wind pierced through Robert's exposed skin. They had taken his coat off at some stage and all he had on now was his pants and shirt, and socks on his feet. His shoes had disappeared as well. It made sense as there was no way he could even think of escaping into the cold without his protective clothing.

The cold air had the effect of clearing his mind a little more and he no longer succumbed to the disorientating effects of the drug. Again he heard no footsteps from those already in the room but he did notice that the atmosphere changed. He assumed it was because someone of higher rank or importance had entered. And he had a sense that his interrogation was about to begin.

Suddenly he felt one of the goons move and his blindfold was ripped off and a bright light shone in his face. He blinked a couple of times and his eyes began to water profusely as they tried to adjust to the light. A man's deep gruff voice filled the smoky air. 'Good morning.'

He was straining to make out shapes, but with the dust reflected in the light, coupled with the fact that his eyes were blurry from the blindfold, he found it a strain. He kept quiet and out of the shadows walked a short, stocky, bearded man well bundled up for the cold weather. His fur hat, or shapka, sat snugly on his head. Slung casually over the man's shoulder was an AK-47 rifle. Without warning he slammed the rifle against Robert's head.

'What!' The exclamation escaped his bloodied lips as he fell to the floor.

A plate crashed to the floor next to him. 'Breakfast. Eat.'

Robert opened one bloodied eye and surveyed the scattered remains of what appeared to be a type of potato. Once more the rifle came down, only this time it came down with a vengeance onto his back. His eyes smarted with the pain. 'I said EAT.'

He edged forward and started to lick the scattered potato from the filth-ridden floor. The potato tasted salty, and he winced once more as the rifle butt slammed into his kidneys. He looked up slyly at his aggressor. The bearded man smiled a toothless smile, then reached behind him and produced a small glass of water. He offered it to his lips and then laughed heartily as he tossed it over Robert's face.

That one sip was not enough, but Robert knew that if he were to lick the floor for the precious drops of water, he would as likely as not pick up some virus which would ultimately make him weaker. And he couldn't have that. He had to remain as strong as he possibly could for as long as he could.

The man left, and suddenly he realised that he was all alone. When had they gone? The sound from the wind outside was gaining momentum and he shivered slightly in his wet shirt. Here he was, sitting in the middle of a room in the middle of Siberia, for all he knew. The light shining down on him was bright. Brighter than necessary, but his eyes were beginning to adjust.

He squinted at his surroundings. There were no windows after all, and only one door. The door to freedom? Or a frozen death? It had to be the latter but either way, he had a strong feeling that he was about to find out. Before they even entered the room he had been aware of their arrival. Their boots had clicked noisily in the sudden silence granted by a reprieve from the wind.

One man was short, one a bit taller, and both looked as if they had been through the wars. And all things considered, they probably had. They both wore thick black jackets and green army pants shoved into their brown snow-covered boots.

The shorter one reached towards him and yanked a blindfold over his eyes, and for one moment he almost betrayed himself with an involuntary turning of the head. The cut across his eye from his recent rendezvous with the AK-47 smarted like hell. They threw a jacket on him and stuffed his feet into some boots that were too big. They didn't bother doing up the laces, so he knew that he would not have them on for long. But why were they bothering with them at all, he wondered?

Together they pulled, punched and dragged him across the floor and through the door to the outside. Robert gulped at the fresh air. At least he could still do that. A shadow passed across his mind and he wondered what time of day it was.

Nobody spoke and Robert tried to count the number of footsteps to where he was going. For all he knew, they were on their way to toss him off a cliff. He could feel the snow under him and knew without a doubt that he was still in Russia and he was probably right with his assumption that he was in Siberia. And in the vastness of Siberia he would probably remain until they killed him. Because he was certain of one thing: they would want him dead when they were finished with him. That is, if they didn't kill him now. His only hope was that it would be quick.

They entered a room and Robert heard the door bang open and closed with aggravated force. He was thrown into a chair. He sniffed, and smelt the aroma of cigar smoke. So, Mr Cigar Breath was here, was he? And who else? There was movement behind him and then to his left, and before he was aware of what was to happen, his head was viciously thrown forward onto the desk.

Gasping, he lifted his head and tasted the iron taste of blood. His nose felt broken and the pain worked its way through his skull. And then the interrogation began.

'What is your name?' The voice betrayed it was a smoker's. In his mind he drew up a picture of a middle-aged man, bald, with fat fingers and perhaps a gold ring on the small one. If he was Russian, as he sounded, then he would probably have a few gold teeth as well.

'Robert.' His voice sounded strong and firm to his ears. Good! That showed them that he was still in control, maybe not of the situation, but of himself.

'What is your family name?' Robert listened closely to his voice and detected a faint trace of another accent. British? Could he be? Robert felt the cold walk of death cross his spine. But he couldn't be, could he? What sense could he make of that if he was right? If this man was indeed British?

'I am not permitted to answer that question.'

'What is your family name?'

'I am not permitted to answer that question.'

He heard the fist slam into the table and Mr Cigar Breath's voice took on an angry and raised tone. 'What is your family name?'

Robert knew what would happen if he failed to answer the question once more.

Mr Cigar Breath eyed the man in front of him, watching with some degree of malice as he tried to regain his composure, and he knew that Robert thought he understood the game that was being played out. That is, if you could call it a game. But he had noticed the slight pause when Robert began to talk. He knew that it was very unlikely that Robert would work out what was really happening here. In fact, there were very few who could. He had planned this operation for so long and in such secret surroundings that it would have amazed him if someone had indeed worked it all out.

He needed information from Robert and he needed it badly. It wasn't just particulars he wanted, it was names. And he wanted to find the faces that matched those names, and then he wanted to make them suffer.

He leant back in his chair, comfortable in the knowledge that they had the right man, he could feel it in his bones; but he would not kill him if he found out that he had had no involvement in the massacre in Donnas. It had taken him years to get to this point. Years. And finally retribution would be his and he would take it. Just as he had taken it with Patrick and the old man. He would eliminate everyone he could that had had any involvement in the death of his only, beloved daughter. At the memory of her, his face clouded over and leaning forward he repeated angrily, 'What is your family name?' Bits of spit erupted from his thin purple lips. His eyes glazed over in an effort to keep the madness at bay. He had to find out names from him and he had to know how deep it actually went. He was beginning to get the feeling that it went far deeper than he had at first imagined, and he was going to push and push Robert until he found out what he wanted to know.

'I am not permitted to answer that question.' Once more his head was slammed into the table and he felt as if he had lost half his hair at the same time.

The questions continued, as did the punishment.

'Where do you work?'

'I am not permitted to answer that question.'

'Where – do – you – work' – each word was clearly stated.

'I am not permitted to answer that question.'

He had to break him if he had any chance of getting anything out of him at all.

Mr Cigar Breath slammed his fists into the table once more and bellowed in Russian, 'Take this piece of scum away and bring him back once you have seen to him.' And in English he leant forward and spat at Robert, 'You will pay, just as the others have done.' Yes, he felt confident that they would get what they wanted from this man. He stretched heartily, enjoying the feeling of pulling each muscle taut. Shaking his head as if to release the demons, he reached across the desk for his cold cup of coffee and took a welcome swig of the black contents, delighting in the bitter taste of hate.

Robert was roughly pulled up from his seat and dragged out into the snow. Fists flew at him from all directions. He huddled there in the snow, not knowing where the punches were coming from or when. Barely conscious, he was pulled and shoved back to the room where Mr Cigar Breath was undoubtedly waiting.

'What is your name?'

'Robert.' His words slurred a little and he shook his head to clear the fast-descending fog.

'What is your family name?' He could hear a cigar being lit and Mr Cigar Breath taking a deep breath. Robert knew that if he ever got out of this, he would forever associate that smell with his ordeal.

'I am not permitted to answer–' But he couldn't finish. The fog enveloped him and he passed out.

When he awoke he found himself back in his room, lying on the bare stone floor. He hands were still tied and as he looked down he realised that the coat and boots had been removed, just as he knew they would be. It was cold in the room. Very cold now, but not freezing.

Against the opposite wall was what looked like a

threadbare blanket. He wormed his way there on his stomach, and tried to twist it around his body, before long falling into a dead sleep.

15

Stuart had just finished a raunchy number and looked up into the night sky. The organisers had arranged a special event at Gorky Park especially for them. They were lucky that the snow had held off and although cold, it was a beautiful night.

There were easily a thousand young fans dancing chaotically in front of them, which surprised them, as they thought not many people would want to come out in the freezing night air. They were probably dancing to keep warm as well as blending in with the rhythm of the songs.

He glanced at Len and watched as he walked to the centre of the stage. He was an excellent musician. His slight frame seemed almost dwarfed by the guitar, but his slim fingers handled the chords majestically. There was no denying his talent when he played like this. He hadn't always got on well with Len – he put it down to personal differences, and different values in their own lives – but they were doing fine now and it had never affected them as a group. And when all was said and done, he liked Len.

While he played, Stuart sat in a corner of the outdoor stage where he would not be easily seen by the crowds below and took a sip of lukewarm tea from a flask provided by the organisers. He wondered, casually, if they could put any vodka in as he was sure that most of the crowd had some degree of vodka coursing through their veins to keep them warm.

Sad Sam and Benjamin joined in with Len, and there followed an incredible mixture of voluptuous music full of rhythm and soul. It always left Stuart moved and he often wondered why they actually needed him. They were the talents, the real musicians, and at times he felt that he was just an accessory to the event. They were the music behind his voice.

As Len played he thought back to his recent actions. It had been quite easy to persuade their manager to arrange a trip here to Moscow. And it had been vitally important to Len that they came to Russia, and in particular Moscow. There was someone he had to see to find out what was going on. There was no telling what was going to happen in the next forty-eight hours, but he felt that he was finally getting somewhere. For a brief moment he lost himself in the music that filled him and forgot his IRA role.

He had been contacted by Patrick, whom he had met, quite by chance, in a small country called The New Independent State of Commans. Since then it had changed its name several times. His involvement there had been a bit tricky, but his ultimate aim of securing aid for terrorism failed dismally when he was betrayed by the Yellow and the Red. He was not too sure how much MI6 knew about his activities there, but he had managed to return to Ireland, change his name and appearance and quite simply lose himself, quite successfully, in his music. But if they had known, they certainly were not paying much attention to him these days.

It did seem strange that he had not heard from Patrick for a while, but he figured there had been a slight delay. They had arranged two meetings; he had not shown up for the first, which could mean that he felt unsafe. They were due to meet tomorrow, though, just before the band left. If he did not turn up tomorrow, then he would forget the whole story and just head back and look for more backing elsewhere. He wondered idly why the FSB wanted his help. But if it proved financially rewarding for the IRA, then he had no complaints. After all, it happened more often than most people knew about or cared to know. One hand neatly helping the other.

He knew without a doubt that the others had no idea at all of what was going on, and he liked it that way. It kept them safe, which on some level it appealed to his disjointed sense of vanity and fairness. And he did *like* them. Although if push ever came to shove, then he would not hesitate to put his own self-preservation first. He was, after all, a selfish man.

His enrolment into the IRA had come about as a result of intense boredom. Having come from a normal family environment, he had completed school successfully and then found himself unemployed, with time weighing heavily on his hands. So he had decided to join the IRA. That was how it had started. No dramatic life-altering event that had intervened and forced him to take up arms. Nothing like that at all; he had just been bored – bored out of his mind.

And, of course, once he had joined he had found his secret life intoxicating. Even when his parents died peacefully and neatly together, they had still no idea of his secret life. He enjoyed keeping it secret, it made him feel powerful.

He carried on playing, enjoying the feel of the taut strings beneath his fingers. Walking around to the front of the stage, he felt that he had the audience in the palm of his hand. His talent as a musician was indisputable and he enjoyed the power that came with it. With his eyes closed he beat out his melody while entranced in his own world, walking his own imaginary path in life.

As he struck the last note, and while the sound was still vibrating around Gorky Park, he fell down dead. The bullet that had gone through his head was now lying aimlessly on stage, covered in brains.

A little bit away from the scene of carnage, a slight, greying man put his hand back into his pocket and walked away smiling contently.

Stuart closed the door behind him and leant against it. He was so tired he could barely move. Stumbling across to his bed he threw himself down, not bothering to change, and fell into a dead sleep. The events of the last few hours seemed so surreal that he just could not believe that they had actually happened. Len was dead, shot right in front of him, and he couldn't get the image of it out of his head. The dribble of blood that splattered out between his teeth. The innocent droplets that chose to gather at the huge void that was once his brain. The smell and the stench of death had penetrated his clothes and into his very being. He welcomed unconsciousness.

16

Nikolai closed his heavy car door behind him with a bang and rested his gloved hands on the black steering wheel, feeling the cold reach his hands through his gloves. It was unusual for him to take his own car to work, but he had decided it would be best if he did, almost as if some hidden instinct had kicked in. It had been a hard and tiring day, and as he sat in the car quietly for a few seconds, he felt glad it was over. He was exhausted and keen to get home.

Yawning, he reached for the ignition to start the car, then froze. A strong hand gripped his arm and a crisp, clear English voice hissed out, 'Don't say a word. Just drive.'

He didn't move a muscle; instead he sat there, wondering what he should do next – if anything. He tried to figure out if the man was armed; if he was, it would be extremely foolish not to do as he was being instructed. Slowly the steel grip of the fingers on his arm was released and he moved his hands back onto the steering wheel. The impression of the man's fingers burned into his skin and he rubbed his arm. Slowly and carefully he turned the key in the ignition. The car started without a hitch. He didn't want to make any sudden moves in case the man in the back seat mistook them and shot him. He had a very clear impression that he would not hesitate to kill him should he have to, and he had no desire to be a corpse just yet.

Slowly and smoothly he backed out of his parking spot, put

on his car lights as it had grown dark and began to edge into the fast-moving traffic. He kept glancing into his rear-view mirror, hoping for a glimpse of the man, but to no avail. Suddenly he felt more than bone weary, and realised that he was in fear of losing the thread of a very convincing theme that he had been mulling over all day. Sighing to himself, he drove quietly and quickly, and eventually they reached the parking lot of the Ramstore Supermarket, just outside the centre of Moscow. It had taken them almost two hours to get there because of the traffic.

The car park was relatively quiet and Nikolai looked in the rear-view mirror and started. There was the reflection of a man who he at first thought was a gangly teenager, but he soon realised on closer inspection that he was much older. This was confirmed as his uninvited guest moved ungainly into the front passenger seat.

'I hope I didn't frighten you?' The voice which had been frightening before took on a soft and pleasant tone.

'No,' he lied blatantly, 'but who are you?' Nikolai was more curious than afraid now as he realised that it was not the intention of the man to kill him.

There was a soft laugh. 'I'm not here to kill you, Nikolai, if that is what you thought.' There was a pause and Nikolai eyed him suspiciously, noticing the tired look around his eyes. The man cleared his throat and looked straight ahead of him as if he were afraid something in his eyes would betray him. 'I'm looking for Robert.'

The name fell onto a heavy silence and seemed to vibrate against the closed confines of the car. 'And I'm stepping so far out of my boundaries to approach you in my search that it is actually laughable,' he finished softly. But Don was not laughing. He would not have taken such a drastic course if it had not been as serious, and he reasoned that Nikolai was probably the only one who would have some idea where Robert was. At least he prayed it was so.

After what seemed an age, Nikolai repeated the name that the stranger had uttered into the silence of the car: 'Robert?' His voice was louder than he had intended and he looked, startled, at his passenger. 'Who the hell are you?' Nikolai tried to gain some control over his crackling voice, but it was only minor. He felt old and almost too weary to carry on.

His passenger continued to stare straight ahead, as if lost in another world. Finally he shrugged his shoulders as if he had reached a conclusion. 'You know,' he began, 'I think that it would be better for you not to know.' He turned to face Nikolai. 'At least for now. But I am a friend and I know that his life is in danger.' The voice grew quiet and gentle. 'And I have to find him before it's too late.' He tried to ignore the thought that he could be too late already.

Nikolai surveyed his passenger and realised that he believed him. Sadly he shook his head. 'I don't know where he is. You have to believe that.' Why did he add that last sentence? he reprimanded himself. It sounded a bit too desperate, a bit too anxious to please, even to his own ears, but he wanted this man to believe him. Desperately. He had to convey in some way that he had no idea where Robert was. He could sense the hidden urgency in his companion, the underlying currents that spoke volumes, even if his passenger did not.

He paused. 'I myself have tried to find him, but all my questions have been met by blank walls.' The man looked out of the window at nothing in particular, and yawned. It had been a hard few days, but Don was determined to find Robert, no matter what it took. He turned to look at Nikolai. 'Or maybe you have the wrong end of the stick and they don't want to kill you.' He sighed – almost as if to himself. 'Maybe there is something else going on.'

Nikolai started. Somehow the idea of something going on that he was unaware of made the whole situation more frightening, but it did make sense in some ridiculous, ludicrous way.

'You could be right. That thought had briefly crossed my mind.' Nikolai's voice sounded hollow, even to his own ears. He looked out into the dark night and focused on the soft flakes falling gently to the ground. He gazed unseeingly at the two young women standing under the bright street lamp. One turned and faced him, and suddenly the light from the street lamp caught the glistening of an object – an object that he knew only too well. He watched, mesmerised, as she raised her arm and pointed – directly at them.

The light seemed to bounce off the pistol as if teasing him. A slow smile of blood-red flooded the woman's face and he almost imagined the leap of joy springing into her eyes. He watched fascinated as her mouth opened wide and she took a silent, deadly aim.

He felt all arms and legs as he sprang into action. Without conscious thought he shot the car to life and began to reverse frantically through the car park, which had begun to fill up. He increased speed and flung the car forward just as a bullet seemed to whizz past his head and smash into the side mirror. The splinters flew up into the night and cascaded viciously onto the silent snow.

He drove like a bat out of hell, continually glancing frantically in his rear-view mirror. Finally he began to slow as he realised that they were not being followed.

'Looks like I'm involved somehow. But with what? Who wants to kill me?' He turned to look at his stony-faced passenger as he stopped quietly under some trees. 'I think that it's time you told me what you know, don't you?' He was sweating with fear and adrenaline, his breath coming in short raspy sounds. Death did not appeal to him. He wanted to retire by the coast and go fishing. He was an appalling fisherman but that did not stop his dream.

His passenger said nothing for a while, then told him, 'I had nothing to do with that, you know.'

Nikolai bit down hard on his bottom lip until he could

taste blood, 'I know.' And somehow he did know. He believed him. Once again he believed this perfect stranger. He stared unseeingly straight ahead of him. They sat quietly for a while, each absorbed in his own thoughts. Nikolai could not pin-point the exact time that his passenger had a change of heart, he just felt it.

The man cleared his throat and looked directly at Nikolai as if he was about to deliver his testimonial. 'Let me introduce myself to you, I'm Don Brett, head of MI6.' Don waited quietly as this information was absorbed by Nikolai. To be fair to him, he seemed to take it quite well, or so Don thought.

Finally Nikolai spoke. 'Well, Mr Brett, we seem to be in a spot of bother and I think that it is time we joined forces and came clean with each other. You tell me what you know, and I will tell you what I know, and together we can, maybe, work out what the hell is going on here!' God, he was tired. He rubbed a hand roughly over his eyes. 'Of course, we now have quite a bit of unwanted attention, so it will make our work a bit more difficult.' Nikolai felt that, although weary, he was once more getting a grip on the situation and, more importantly, himself.

Don nodded. 'Why did they wait until now to make their move?' He looked at Nikolai questioningly and the other shrugged his shoulders. 'Did you notice if you were being followed at all?'

'No, I didn't.' Nikolai gave an ironic smile. 'I was more concerned with my passenger in the back seat! And besides,' he continued, 'I have done nothing unusual during the last few days.' He sat there thinking quietly for a while, going over the events of the last few days, and then suddenly a small bubble of fear began to spread out from the bottom of his stomach, making him feel physically ill. 'Oh my God!' he mumbled softly to himself, and he turned a pale face to Don.

'What? What is it? Tell me?' Don urged

'I did a small favour for a friend of mine.' He swallowed hard. ' I arranged for a group, a small pop group to play at Gorky.' He paused and stared out into the dark forest that surrounded them. 'And last night one of their members was killed. A bullet straight through the brain. Quite a mess, apparently.' His thoughts wandered idly back to the previous night's happenings.

Don was instantly alert and grabbed at Nikolai's arm. 'Which band member?' His voice was raised, even to his own ears.

'Len. He was the guitarist.'

'Len!' Nikolai heard the released pent-up breath of air escape Don. 'Thank God!' He looked at Nikolai, who seemed to be waiting for some sort of explanation. 'Quite ironic that really,' Don continued, almost as if to himself. 'A terrorist who meets his end in the same way he has killed hordes of others. I only wish that he could have suffered more, but I suppose that he did get his just deserts after all. But what was he doing here? Someone must have contacted him with a very lucrative deal or he would not have made the trip.'

Nikolai sighed. 'Yes, I think that you are right there. And I believe that it was perhaps Patrick – one of our agents and, as it turns out, one of yours – that contacted him.'

Don looked puzzled and a bit taken aback. 'No – no, that can't be right. Patrick was working on something else. It had nothing to do with the IRA.' He looked directly at Nikolai. 'I know what he was working on, so someone else must have contacted him on the pretext of being Patrick. But for heaven's sake why? What the hell is going on here?'

Silent swirls of fear twisted around both Don and Nikolai as they sat, once more silent, in the dark car, trying to fathom out the whole mess. And in the midst of it all, with his head pounding nineteen to the dozen, Don kept hoping fervently that they would find Robert – alive.

17

Elizabeth walked towards her grey apartment block with a shiver. It was bitterly cold and she rubbed her hands together and blew some rather ineffective lukewarm air onto her gloves. Her fingers remained frozen and she buried them back deep into the pockets of her fur coat while snuggling her face and ears down into the thick woollen scarf round her neck. Her hat was pulled down low over her eyes and it cast a deep shadow across her face in the late watery afternoon sun.

She stamped her boots onto the cold metal rungs of the door mat that stood alone and isolated at the entrance to her bleak apartment block. There were men on the roof just opposite, scraping the ice off to prevent it falling and killing someone when the weather warmed up. The sound of the thick blocks of ice falling onto the soft snow nearby barely registered. She placed a gloved hand on the doorknob and pushed it open. It was dark inside and she figured, accurately, that the light bulb had blown once more.

She had moved here the night after her attack. No one knew of her 'safe' place, or at least that is what she thought. But she was not a fool and had already contacted the British Embassy, where she worked in Chancery as a registry clerk, to tell them that she would not be in for a few days. That gave her some cover and some time to finalise her departure from Moscow as she could not leave until she had tied up a few loose threads. Which thankfully would not take long. Things had become just a little bit too precarious for her to remain here at the moment.

With her right gloved hand, she gingerly felt for the stair rail that ran along the rotten wall on her right. Climbing the three cold stone steps, she made her way to the barely visible light of the lift. The sound of her boots echoed loudly in the silent corridor.

Her thoughts were miles away as she reached towards the iron gate and pushed it aside. The sudden brightness in the lift made her eyes water. She was weary and beginning to feel a little sorry for herself. Hunching herself together, she shivered and pressed the button for the fourth floor. The doors closed almost too noisily and the lift made its creaky way upwards, jerking to a sudden halt. Absently she pushed the lift doors open and stepped out, only to realise that she had made a mistake and climbed out on the wrong floor. A small frown etched her brow as she figured that she must have pushed the wrong button as she was now on the fifth floor. The pale light of the fast fading sun filtered sulkily through the dirty window at the end of the corridor and did nothing to warn her of her impending doom.

Shivering, she decided to walk the fifteen uneven stone steps to the floor below. Reaching her door, she ignored the peeling paint and inserted her key into the rusty lock. Stepping over the doorframe, she reached with her right hand towards the light cord and pulled it.

The apartment flooded with light. It was sparsely furnished as she had no need for anything more than the basics. From the front door you could look out over the small lounge with three weary worn couches placed randomly around. They were orange with broad green stripes. Not exactly her favourite but they would do for the meantime. She had drawn the moth-ridden brown curtains before she went out, so no outside light filtered into the apartment.

It wasn't a very nice apartment, but it would serve its purpose for the next few days as she made her final preparations to leave.

She took off her gloves and coat and flung them onto a nearby chair. Sitting down on the armrest of the chair, she removed her boots and left them there as she walked into the kitchen in her socks for a drink. She pulled out a half bottle of wine from the fridge and poured some into the glass that she had left on the small draining board the previous evening.

Leaning back, she sighed as she raised the glass to her lips. After a while she pushed her weary body up and walked back into the lounge and knew instinctively that something was wrong. As she looked cautiously around the small lounge, she saw him sitting – facing her. Beaming at her almost like a big, fat Cheshire cat. A horrible blob of a man. He just sat and said nothing while he watched her. A thousand emotions seemed to cross her face all at once. Should she run for it? If she did, would she be successful? She doubted it. He had already tried to kill her once, and she knew that he would not let her escape so easily the second time.

She walked slowly but with a purpose towards the couch which faced him and sat down. Every move that she made was made with a purpose and not once did she take her eyes off him. By God she hated him! His slimy, horrible personality made her feel physically ill.

Her composure seemed to unnerve him just a little, but he smiled even more broadly. 'Hello, Elizabeth. Surprised to see me?' he mocked.

Slowly she placed the glass on the table beside her. 'What do you want, Barry? To finish me off?' His cruel, callous laughter vibrated around her apartment and her brain. 'You're a bastard!' she spat at him.

He leaned towards her. 'Yeah, you're probably right,' he hissed at her between his teeth. 'But you – you're a bitch of the highest order, and I am not about to repeat my mistake.' She shivered at the cold, heartless tone in his voice.

She stood up and angrily faced him. 'You're a coward!' she accused him. 'You didn't even have the courage to do things yourself last time – what makes you think you could do it this time?'

'You bitch!' He flew out of his chair in a rage and flung himself on her, taking her unawares. As they fell to the floor, he grabbed her throat with one hand and pressed for dear life. Gasping for breath, she could feel the veins bursting in her brain as she struggled for air. She managed to free herself briefly, and as she flung her arms above her head, the small silver blade that Barry had contrived to get out of his pocket ripped through her. She gasped in pain and Barry, feeling victorious and redeemed, lifted himself off her with a hollow laugh. He stood looking down at her as she gasped in pain like a wounded animal.

Smiling contently to himself, he watched as she lay there, suffering, until she grew silent. He knew she was going to die and it pleased his evil, vicious mind that she would die in pain and agony. He raised his boot and kicked her silent body and left. His job was done, the secret secure. Pulling his coat up around his ears, he walked back to his car.

John Masters sat in the pub with his head despondently between his hands, thinking that life could not possibly get more dreary. Raising his eyes to his glass, he watched as a water droplet silently formed and then ran gently down the glass to be absorbed by the soaking-wet placemat beneath it. Sighing loudly, he raised the glass to his lips and took a deep, nourishing glug of his beer, then looked across at the equally dismal face of Ian Pilchard, who sat drinking with him.

Ian raised his glass lethargically from his placemat and

sipped the cool, golden liquid. His pale blue eyes, hidden from view behind thick glasses, glanced across at John. He admired John's dark, almost chocolately good looks. He had recently shaved off his moustache which, according to Ian, was a good move on John's part as the fur on the top of his lip had made him look just a tad silly. Ian rubbed his hands through his strawberry blond hair and raised his eyes questioningly at another sigh from John.

'You all right there mate?' he asked curiously.

'Yeah,' John sighed again. 'Wonder if I should go skating later. Care to join me?'

'Sounds tempting, but no – best not.' He took another sip of his drink. 'You know how jealous William gets, and besides, are you well enough to go skating?'

'Yip, doc says it was just a nasty viral thing, but I'm fine now,' John mumbled almost to himself, shrugging off the horrible memory of feeling so ill and sorry for himself.

They sat for a few more moments in companionable silence, which was broken suddenly by the sharp ringing of John's cell-phone. The typically English pub that they had found in the middle of Moscow was almost deserted. It was close enough to the British Embassy, where they both worked, for them to come for a quick lunch or a drink at the end of the day. At times there were quite a few of them there having a casual drink before heading home, but tonight it was just the two of them.

John reached casually for his phone and, pressing the green OK button, answered it. Ian sat quietly opposite, staring at their reflection in the dirty windows. Idly he ran his finger down the window, watching the small line it left behind. Slowly he became aware of the terse conversation taking place across from him.

'Elizabeth?' There was a pause, 'Elizabeth, is that you? I can barely hear you? What? What?' He gesticulated wildly at Ian for a pen and paper. 'Yes – yes, I am writing it down.' John wrote furiously with his left hand on a discarded placemat. 'I'll be with you as soon as I can – just hold on.'

John flipped his phone closed with agitated fingers. 'I'm sorry, Ian,' he mumbled as he rose hastily from the warm chair he had occupied for the last hour, 'but I have to dash…' Ian barely caught John's last words as he watched him fly out of the pub, grabbing his thick winter coat as he went.

Ian sat looking after him and wondered briefly to himself what the hell was going on. Thoughtfully he raised his glass to his lips and drained it in one swift motion. Pushing it to one side, he got up and left the pub, hoping to himself that by the time he got home, William would have prepared dinner.

John reached the address that Elizabeth had given him within a matter of ten minutes. He took the stairs two at a time as he flew towards her apartment. On the way there he had called an ambulance.

Reaching her apartment, he leant against the door and it gave way. The light almost blinded him after the dark passage and entrance hall to this rather dingy looking apartment. But his eyes adjusted quickly as he focused on the still form of Elizabeth lying against a rather mangy-looking couch.

He raced over and leant over her, fearful that she was already dead. 'Elizabeth?' She barely moved. Very gently he removed the phone that was clutched in her bloodied fingers and lifted her gently onto the couch. She moaned slightly and for a moment he hoped that she would be OK, but as he looked at her he realised that there was no hope. A pool of blood covered her top, and blood had congealed in between her fingers. 'Elizabeth?' he whispered hoarsely once more.

She moved her head towards the sound of his voice. 'John?' Her voice was threadbare and he leant closer to her mouth to catch her words.

'It's all right. I'm here now.' He leant closer to her ear so that she could hear him. 'Don't talk. The ambulance is on its way.' And he added, 'You're going to be OK,' but the assurances were merely for him, and they both knew it.

He had worked with her for two years now and he had grown very fond of her. They hadn't as yet been out on a date, but he had hoped that they soon would. Now that hope would remain unfulfilled.

She opened her eyes and stared directly at him. 'John.' She was barely audible now. 'Robert Brown – missing.' She was gasping for air, desperate for him to hear and understand what she had to say. 'Barry – you have to find – find…' She struggled on, 'Don't – don't.' Her voice was painfully thin and wispy and he had to lean close to her, trying to reassure her, encouraging her to keep her strength. But she was determined to tell him what she needed to. 'Barry – don't trust…' Her eyes bulged with concentration but it was already too late. Her sentence remained unfinished as he watched the light leach out of her beautiful eyes. Grabbing her, he held her for what seemed ages. Only when the gentle hand of an ambulance paramedic touched his shoulder did he dare move.

'She's gone now,' they assured him gently in Russian. But he hadn't needed them to tell him that. He knew just by her eyes. There was no life left in her at all and he watched helplessly as they lifted her onto a trolley and covered her with a white sheet. Silently the blood from Elizabeth's soaked clothes worked its way through the white sheet, staining it. It seemed as if, in some macabre way, she was sending him a silent message.

There would be questions, he knew that, and he wished desperately that he knew the answers.

As he walked towards the door to go, he saw a small white piece of paper lying on the floor. Idly he bent down to retrieve it. Glancing at it, he read the name *Stuart Love* and a contact number. Thoughtfully he put the crumpled piece of paper into his pocket and, turning off the lights, closed the apartment door. There was nothing more he could do there tonight.

18

Stuart woke with a thumping headache. Moaning, he rolled over and covered his aching face with the softness of the pillow, but it was absolutely useless. Removing the pillow, he opened one eye cautiously and saw the room spin in front of him. Hastily he closed it again. He felt like death. In fact, he was sure that death would be preferable to this.

As if by some cruel joke, the phone next to his bed began to shrill loudly, taunting him and his fragile state. The ear-piercing ring seemed to bounce around his tired, alcohol-soaked brain. Viciously, with one sweep of his arm Stuart flung it off the table and onto the ground, where it came to rest in a disturbing array of broken pieces. Aah! Silence. Putting his head beneath the blankets, he tried to bury himself once more into unconsciousness. It was useless. The pounding in his head just would not go away.

He was almost in tears as he dragged himself up and into the bathroom. Cursing with every agonising step, he promised to himself that he would never, ever drink again, no matter what the circumstances were. Grabbing for any painkiller that he could find, he swallowed five and stumbled back to bed, convinced that his fellow band members were in a similar state of disrepair.

It felt like a mere two seconds later when there was banging on his room door. At first it took him a while to figure out where the awful booming sound was coming from, and as he began to make sense of the noise, he cautiously opened his eyelids once more to find out that it was lighter in the room.

Leaning over towards the small table next to him he searched for his watch. It wasn't on the table and he looked down at the floor. There it was, lying among the broken pieces of the phone. Reaching down, he pulled it towards him and glanced casually at the time. It was now half past two in the afternoon, and somehow that bothered him.

The banging continued, but it was now accompanied by a softly spoken male voice. 'Mr Love? Are you there?' A short pause. 'Mr Love?' Some more banging. God! This man was persistent! 'Mr Love! It is urgent that I speak with you!' It was obvious that the man wouldn't go away until he had seen him.

'Yeah, OK! Give me a minute!' He looked around for the white complimentary robe, which had been flung casually on a chair by the window, got up carefully, as the pain-killers had not seemed to have made much difference, and made his way cautiously towards the door. After the night that he had just had, he couldn't possibly believe that things could get worse. He was wrong. He knew that the moment he opened the door.

'What now?' he almost bellowed. 'Are you from the police again? I told you that there was no more that I could do for you!' He felt like adding, 'So fuck off' but refrained just in time, which was surprising even for him.

John surveyed the unkempt, dishevelled figure in front of him, twitching his nose ever so slightly at the stench of stale booze.

'Mr Love, why would you think I was from the police? Are you in some kind of trouble?' The voice was pleasant enough, and through the hazy thumping of his head, he realised that it was English.

'Oh crikey! I'm sorry, but after last night, things just

seemed to be spiralling out of control. So, I just assumed…' He left the sentence unfinished, lamely.

'Mr Love.' John cut him short as he was not in the least bit interested in what happened 'last night'. He had his own problems to deal with. 'I am not from the police, but I do need to talk to you.' He paused as if to add emphasis to his next few words. 'It really is very important, Mr Love. *Very important.*'

Stuart looked at him through a haze. Somehow the last sentence seemed to be penetrating the fog around his brain. 'Why? If it isn't about Len?' He seemed a bit confused now, as he stood with one hand on the cold brass knob, looking up at this very good-looking dark-haired stranger whose shirt looked ruffled and his face unshaven and his eyes just a little bit sad.

'Mr Love, my name is John Masters and I am here from the British Embassy, and I really need to talk to you. Here is my card.' He handed Stuart his business card and Stuart gave it a cursory glance. 'Please, Mr Love, all will be clear if we could just have a chat.' He indicated the room behind Stuart. 'I think that it would be a good idea if you got dressed and then maybe we could have some coffee somewhere?'

Stuart suddenly felt too tired to figure out what was going on and sulkily muttered, 'Sure, why not?' He retreated into his room. 'Come in and wait while I have a shower and clean up.'

John followed him into the room and walked over to the window, standing with his back to Stuart. He put his hands in his pockets and hunched his shoulders, thinking. Stuart watched him silently for a few moments and then stumbled off to the shower, slamming the door behind him.

John turned slightly at the sound of the bathroom door closing and carried on with his thoughts. He had to find out what Stuart knew – if anything. He heard the sound of the shower being turned on and figured it was just as well, as the stench of stale booze had been appalling.

Stuart was dressed and ready in fifteen minutes, and with his sunglasses firmly in place made his way, together with John, towards the lift.

'Can I ask what this is all about?' Stuart asked curiously on the way down.

'Not now, Mr Love. Patience – please.' He seemed vaguely irritated with Stuart, which in fact he was as his train of thought had been broken by Stuart's question.

Together they walked into the restaurant, which was practically empty, and sat down together quietly in a corner. 'As you know, I'm from the British Embassy and –'

But before he could carry on Stuart interrupted, 'It's about time you guys got here! It was absolute murder when Len got shot. We spent hours at the FSB headquarters before they finally let us go, and not a word from you guys.' He paused and took a sip of his lukewarm watery coffee and gagged slightly.

'Mr Love, what are you talking about?' John was confused, and he honestly did not have the time to be sidetracked! He needed whatever information he could get from this man, and he needed it now. Was the man sitting opposite him a bit barmy? He'd heard that you become like that when fame strikes.

'Mr Love indeed! Call me Stuart,' he continued. 'Don't tell me you guys don't know about Len being shot in front of all those fans at Gorky Park? The police told me that they had contacted you, but no one from the Embassy bothered to disturb their beauty sleep to come out to see what was going on!' He took another sip of his rather awful coffee, and continued, 'They put it down to some crazy fanatic – at least, that's their explanation. It should by now be all over the papers, and the news.' Gripping his head, he pulled out more aspirin from his pocket. 'Shit! My fucking head hurts!' He swallowed the pills with some force.

'Stuart, I'm sorry, but I had not heard.' John rubbed a

weary hand over his eyes. 'And, as this is Russia, it does not surprise me that it is neither on the TV nor in the papers.' He looked over at a very green-looking Stuart.

'What the hell is going on here? And if you don't know about Len, what do you want?' he almost shouted. He felt ill, his head hurt and he was beginning to feel totally irritated. 'I have to lie down, mate. I feel just ghastly.' Stuart made as if to leave.

John's restraining hand held him in place. 'No, you can't go. Not yet. There's too much at stake.' He gave Stuart a sweet, cold smile. 'And you're going nowhere until you have helped me.'

'Listen, mate, I don't care who you are, but if I don't go and lie down now, I'm going to puke all over you!' He figured that he had been as decent as could be expected of him in his state, and he was now going to leave.

John leant forward and Stuart stared into a pair of dead-black eyes. His voice, so pleasant a few minutes ago, was now harsh and menacing. 'Mr Love, I am not asking you to help me, I'm telling you. And in this case, you have no choice.' The words were spat out at him with some force.

Stuart swallowed the rising nausea and John continued, 'You will help me, because if you don't help me, more people will die, and before the day is over, your life might just have been added to that list. Now go to the toilet, where you can put your blasted finger down your throat, and then maybe we can get down to some work!'

Silence filled the air as John finished talking, with each staring at the other. Finally Stuart could no longer ignore the queasiness in his stomach and forced out one word 'Fine!' before dashing off to the men's room.

John waited for Stuart outside the toilets, not trusting him out of his sight for long. And it was while he waited that he phoned around. It didn't take him long to get the full picture of what happened with Len. He stood there quietly, frowning, and finally he nodded to himself. The picture was clear now and he knew what he would have to do. From now there would be no going back. It took a while, but eventually a green-faced Stuart emerged and John breathed a quiet word of thanks, knowing, or rather hoping, that Stuart would be able to help him find out why Elizabeth had died. His eyes smarted at the thought of a wasted life, a life with so much promise and so much to live for, brutally taken away. But he could not afford to get sentimental, so he hastily brushed these thoughts from his mind, focusing once more on the man in front of him, who, if he had to be honest, did not look well at all.

'Let's go back to your room to fetch your coat and boots and then you must come with me.' John spoke as if he did not expect to be ignored. He was tired of being pleasant. Was it only last night that he was sighing and saying how nothing happened any more? A few hours was all it took to shatter him to the core, and how he wished that he could turn the clock back. He rubbed a hand over his stomach, feeling a little off-colour himself. The doctor had said that the virus would take a while to leave his system completely.

'Yeah, great, order me around.' Stuart sounded sullen, but went with John anyway, as he figured that compliance would get him to bed quicker than if he tried to rid himself of John.

Soon they were back downstairs and making their way out of the hotel. Turning right, they walked on without speaking for a while. Finally Stuart broke the silence. 'Where are we going?'

'We're going back to my place,' was the crisp reply. 'But before we get there, we need to talk.'

Stuart nodded abstractedly while reaching into his pocket for a cigarette. Lighting it with a packet of rather dismal-looking matches, he inhaled contentedly. He had almost given up smoking but the events of the last few hours had sent him running back for his cigarettes.

'I told you all I know about Len being shot.'

John looked him full in the face. 'This isn't just about Len!' He was getting more and more exasperated with Stuart. 'Are you telling me that in all the time the band has been together, not once, not once during that whole time, did you know that your band mate and "best friend" worked for the IRA?' he asked sarcastically, all his efforts to be diplomatic discarded – and for the moment he did not care. He had to find out about Elizabeth, and the sooner the better.

Stuart stopped dead in his tracks with a startled expression on his face. 'What? What the hell are you talking about?' He started walking again, hastily. 'You must be mad! Stark raving barmy!' he shouted at John, waving his arms around madly in frustration, nearly bumping into an old lady slowly carrying her bundle of bread. His head was thumping and the pain just did not seem to ease. This was like a bad idea, or rather it felt like his worst nightmare.

John ran after him and grabbed his arm. 'Wait, you idiot!'

'Why? So you can chuck more false allegations at me? Insult my intelligence again?' He viciously pulled his arm away. 'Don't you think I would have known? Don't you think I would have guessed?' He was furious now. Who did this John Masters think he was, anyway? He was not a stupid man. He would have known – surely he would have known! How could he not know? Oh my God! Could it be true?

John's next words stopped him cold. 'Precisely. One has to ask the question why didn't you know? Or did you?'

Stuart turned an incredulous face towards John. 'How dare you! How dare you assume that I knew what he was up to! That is, if what you are telling me is indeed *true*!' He flung out the last sentence with such force that he nearly spat on John.

John grabbed his arm again and held on, forcing Stuart to face him. 'Have you ever heard of a place called Donnas, you idiot?'

Pure anguish filled Stuart as he glared uncomprehendingly at John for a second. The pain of a distant memory flooded his mind and before he could stop himself he took a swipe at John. But John, expecting this reaction, took a side step and Stuart fell on his knees into the snow. 'You bastard.' His voice was very quiet, all fight out of him. John had hit him on the one weak spot that he had. His one vulnerability.

'Come on – get up.' John's voice was gentle. 'There's a bench over there that we can sit on. We really do need to talk.'

Stuart got up slowly and brushed the tears from his cheeks with the back of his glove. Tears he didn't even know he had shed until he felt their cold moisture on his face.

They walked in silence to the bench. Brushing the snow off, they both sat down. John stared straight ahead while Stuart sat there, shoulders hunched, looking down.

John could sense the pain that Stuart felt as it oozed out of his very being, but at the same time he realised that he did not have the time to be diplomatic or to tread carefully. He absolutely had to get to the bottom of this mess before it was too late. So he jumped in head first, hoping Stuart wouldn't ask how he knew all the stuff that he was about to acknowledge knowing.

'I know about Anne, Stuart. I know that she died when things got out of control in Donnas.' Stuart said nothing, staring straight down in front of him. 'But what you don't know is about Len's involvement with the uprising,' he continued softly, trying to break this news to Stuart as gently as possible.

Stuart continued to say nothing. 'It gets complicated, but the bits that concern you are the bits that involve Len. He had just recently been recruited by the IRA and he had to organise some funding. He was assured that should he persuade the IRA to "assist" certain governments in a second revolution in the New Independent State of Commas, then the IRA would get some additional funds.'

Stuart stirred slightly. 'What exactly are you saying?' He felt icy cold. The betrayal of a friend who had seen him through his worst and best moments seemed almost incredible to him at this moment.

'I am not saying, I am telling you that Len was indirectly responsible for the death of Anne Greeves.' He stopped and looked at Stuart. 'Of course,' he added, 'to give him credit, he had no idea that Anne would be killed.' He paused as if to add impact to his next words. 'But he did nothing to get her out of there before things exploded – and he got his money. There are a lot of people involved, a lot of governments.'

Stuart lifted his head unbelievingly. 'So, he was shot because he was IRA?' He just couldn't bring himself to hate Len at this stage. He just felt numb.

John smiled to himself. 'No – you see, that is the irony of the whole thing. I believe that Len was shot because Anne died. Because he did nothing to get her out; in other words, he did nothing to save her. He was in effect assassinated by someone who cared very deeply about Anne.'

As the words slowly began to sink in, Stuart started. 'You don't mean...?' He stared, aghast, straight at John. 'You don't mean me? I didn't know about his involvement, I swear.' His eyes clouded and he doubled over, mumbling so softly that John had to lean forward to hear what he was saying. 'But if I had, yes I would have killed him. I loved her. I loved her more than life itself.' He swallowed hard. The cold of the bench was beginning to work itself through to his bones and he shivered. Raising his head, he looked directly at John.

'I know,' John said. 'I believe that if you had known, you would have killed him long ago.' They sat in silence as the ice swirled around their boots. Finally John said, haltingly, 'But –

but there is a further complication that has come to light.' He continued cautiously, trying to put the memory of Elizabeth into perspective; trying to forget seeing the light die from her eyes, 'A woman has been killed. And you knew her.'

'What are you talking about? Which woman?' He had only been in Russia a very short time and what John was saying seemed improbable: that he could be involved in another death. He pulled himself together, but he still looked very pale. Everything was beginning to feel just a little surreal.

'Her name was Elizabeth and she had a piece of paper in her flat with your name and number on it.'

Stuart was beginning to feel deathly ill. 'Elizabeth? Yes, I knew her, but only briefly,' he stammered. 'But what do you mean – dead?'

'She died last night in my arms, Stuart. Someone stabbed her.'

Stuart looked aghast into John's eyes and saw nothing there. No betrayal of any emotion. No sadness, just an emptiness. 'No, that can't be!' he was horrified. 'She said it was just superficial! She walked out of my life alive, I swear!' He finished lamely, 'She said she would be all right. She said she would, otherwise I would never have let her go.' How could he have let this happen? he reprimanded himself fiercely. He felt certain that he could have protected her, kept her safe! In his mind's eye, the picture of Elizabeth was beginning to fuse with that of Anne.

When John next spoke, it took a while for his words to penetrate the grey fog around Stuart's brain. 'She was fine when she left you, Stuart.' John swallowed hard. 'But some bastard wanted to finish off what he had started.' Briefly he closed his eyes as if trying to erase the memory of her death in his arms only a few hours earlier.

This fleeting display of pain was not lost on Stuart. 'Oh, God! I'm so sorry. Was she a friend of yours?' he asked with genuine concern on his ash-grey face.

'No, but she was someone I liked,' John continued quietly. 'Someone I liked a lot.' He was not about to add that both he and Elizabeth had been special agents of Her Majesty's MI6. That was only on a need-to-know basis, and Stuart did not need to know. At least not yet.

Stuart looked at him. 'She came to me one night, scared out of her wits. It seemed that the Russians were after her. She didn't tell me much. In fact she didn't get around to telling me anything. We changed her hair colour and cut it short.'

John nodded quietly. 'Yeah, I noticed. She worked for the Embassy, just like I do.'

Stuart was puzzled. 'But why would she need to change her appearance if they knew where she worked?'

'I don't know, Stuart. I don't know,' John added wearily.

'But why was she killed? As far as I know she had nothing to do with Len, or am I wrong again?' His words were heavy with the bitter irony of the situation. 'Or was it an inside job?' He inhaled deeply, and the fresh air helped a little with his nausea.

John shivered at the implication of Stuart's last statement. In a quiet voice he put forward his idea. 'I believe that she was killed because of the involvement of a certain government in Donnas. In fact, I am almost certain of it. Elizabeth was very clever and I'm almost sure that she was connecting the dots as to exactly what happened there. There is one person who would have signed some incriminating papers – someone who is very anxious to keep their involvement quiet.' He finished, 'And that is why she was killed. And I believe that more are going to die as that someone tries to clean up their past. In their eyes, we cannot be allowed to connect the dots.'

They sat in silence for a while, each trying to absorb the new information.

'For the time being, if it suits you, I would like you to come and stay with me as we have to work this out.'

Stuart nodded silently in agreement. He couldn't stop Anne or Elizabeth from being killed, but he felt he owed it to both of them to find out why, and in so doing he could hopefully put some precious ghosts to rest.

They both rose leaving the stone cold bench behind them to the elements.

19

Mr Cigar Breath sat at his desk, surveying Robert, who sat blindfolded opposite him. As he sat there quietly, he pulled his thin hands together in an agitated state, twisting his fingers to and fro, to and fro. A tiny shadow of doubt fell across his face. Had he been wrong? Did this man know absolutely nothing? He rubbed a cigar-stained finger across his strained forehead, trying for a moment to rub away the memories that haunted him. He would give it a few more days and that was all. He had been so certain – so very certain. No – he shook his head – he had to be right. But he knew his own thoughts lacked conviction.

Robert sat still. He had no idea that some sort of silent debate was going on in front of his blindfold. He had been pulled and tugged reluctantly towards the interrogation room a few minutes earlier, and was now ready for a new round.

His perception of days and times had become distorted, but that was not the only thing. He knew in moments of clarity that he was beginning to lose it. Would he survive? Hopefully. But he doubted that he would ever be the same again.

Robert could not see the pain etched into the man's face opposite him. A man who would, against all odds, get the answers that he was looking for. He had to. Revenge consumed him and ate at every fibre of his living body. He was determined to seek out and kill every last person alive who was responsible for putting the pain there. In his need for vengeance he didn't care about the innocent who could lose their lives along the way. He really didn't care. In fact all he cared about was the truth: the real truth that he knew had to be out there somewhere.

'What is your name?' The questions had begun once again. But this time, Robert answered. It was pointless holding out any more over something that they already knew.

'Robert. My name is Robert.' His voice was dull and emotionless, and the defiance that he had displayed earlier a thing of the past. Something which did not go unnoticed by his captors. Mr Cigar Breath got up quietly from his chair and leant against the far wall. A thick shadow had been cast around the room due to the poor lighting, and only the bottom half of his body could be seen properly, encased in rough brown trousers which were far too big for him and held in place with a frayed old piece of rope. But Robert didn't have to see to begin to feel that the atmosphere had shifted slightly. Had the mere acknowledgement of his name done that? And if it had, why exactly was he here?

They made all the right noises and sounds for terrorists trying to interrogate him, but at times it seemed almost as if it was a bit put on. As if there was something else going on that he did not know about. Maybe they were just going to wear him down until they figured he had reached the end of his tether, and then they would ask him what they really wanted to know. If that was the case, he was very nearly there, and then he would know why he was here. And hopefully he would know it before he died. He knew, too, that when he reached the end, he would give them what they asked. He was no hero and he could only take so much. And to be honest, where was the glory in being a dead hero?

'Robert.' Mr Cigar Breath turned the name around and around on his tongue. He seemed extremely satisfied. Those in the room watched him eagerly, almost drooling in their anticipation that *this time* this interview would lead them to the success that they so desperately sought, and that the madman would move on.

'Robert.' The name was repeated once more. 'I need to ask you a few questions, *Robert.*' Robert shivered as he felt the breath of his tormentor on his face. He had walked so silently that Robert had not realised how close he was to him until he had begun to speak. His cold breath smelled of old coffee and garlic, and Robert shivered involuntarily.

'Who do you work for, Robert?'

Robert was beginning to feel as if his name was being overused and frowned in irritation. 'I cannot answer that question,' he sighed in exasperation, bone weary. His mind wandered off to his bed back in good old safe England. A place where he had always felt safe – his little home, well looked after by his gorgeous wife. He imagined the cool, crisp, clean green and white linen that made up his bed and the welcome feel of his wife next to him. That is what he needed – his bed and his wife.

'It doesn't actually matter, you know – because we know.' There was a deathly silence after this statement as Robert's consciousness was brought screaming back to the present. 'Take him back to his room!'

This made no sense at all! Robert was hoisted up, unprotesting now, by two huge, burly figures. Or at least that is what they felt like. Dragging him across the snow, they reached his room and thrust him back inside. One knelt down next to him as he landed on the cold floor, and removed the bonds that held his hands together. They left the blindfold on for him to remove when they had gone. Slamming the door behind them, they turned the key in the lock. Something they hadn't bothered with until now. Slowly he sat up and removed his blindfold. Sitting there with his knees pulled up to his chin, he began to wonder, once more, what this was all really about, but thoughts of his warm welcome home in England kept intruding.

Mr Cigar Breath sat once more at the table in the middle of the room. The single lit lamp left him partially in shadow and he sat there quietly, very pleased with himself. Now, for the first time, he had no doubt that he would get what he wanted. And he continued to sit there with a quiet, sad, satisfied smile on his face.

20

Don and Nikolai had spent the better part of the evening talking and formulating their plan. It was imperative that they get back into Moscow without being seen, and the sooner the better.

Don knew of one agent in the British Embassy that he had to make contact with. He knew that he could trust her. Elizabeth was one of his best agents and she was bound to have made progress with the disappearance of Robert Brown. She had always had her own method of securing and scouring out the information that was needed and it had proved most successful in the past.

Turning in his seat, Don faced Nikolai. 'What we have to do now, is to try and get into the British Embassy without being seen.'

Nikolai nodded in agreement beneath his fur hat. 'Yes, you're right. If we can do that, then perhaps we can find out more about this situation and try to make some sort of sense of it.'

'I'm in your hands, Nikolai,' Don said quietly, swallowing a ball of uninvited saliva which had gathered in his mouth.

Nikolai sat quietly for a moment and looked unseeing straight ahead of him. Finally he turned to Don. 'I think I know the best way to do it. First, we must drive back to the Kremlin.' Nikolai paused reflectively. 'I know that it is risky, but it is probably our best chance at the moment.' He continued in a quiet voice, 'Once we get there, there are always hordes of tourists, so we park the car by Red Square.'

It was getting colder in the car and Nikolai's breath filmed out in a fan around him. He knew that they would not be able to sit there for much longer, unless they wanted to freeze to death.

'Once we are there, we can mingle amongst the tourists and cautiously make our way across the bridge to the Embassy. That will be the next tricky bit, but once we are across the bridge we can make our way to the small park behind the Embassy and then enter the Embassy via a tunnel that I know of which will take you right into the grounds without being seen.' He turned to Don. 'What do you think?'

Don shrugged and glanced out of their window at the frozen surroundings, working through Nikolai's idea in his head. 'Its worth a shot, but is there no other way into the Embassy?'

Nikolai shook his head. 'No, it'll have to be this way – unfortunately, for the sake of speed. Let's hope that we're not seen.'

'I'll second that,' said Don quietly.

The car was slow to start up in the cold and it took three attempts before it finally sprang into life. They had not dared leave it running in case someone spotted them or heard the noise.

Looking cautiously around them, they edged slowly out of their hiding place. They kept the car lights dim, just enough to see by. Their progress was slow to begin with, but it wasn't long before they joined a small bubbling throng of cars making their way into Moscow, hopefully with some degree of safety.

Both Don and Nikolai cast frequent, anxious glances around to see if they were being followed, but thankfully all seemed safe and they managed to arrive and park near Red Square without being hindered in any way.

Opening the car doors, they gave the scene before them a thorough look and, not noticing any undue attention focused on them, joined a fairly large and noisy group of tourists that was just entering Red Square. The stones were icy and they trod carefully, afraid that one of them might slip and fall, thereby drawing attention to themselves. They moved around with the group for about fifteen minutes before slowly disengaging themselves and carefully making their way towards the bridge that connected the two sides of the road across the river.

Fresh snow had begun to fall softly around them as they walked quickly across the bridge, their journey slightly disguised by quite a few stragglers. They almost didn't notice the two youths who sat hidden in a corner of the bridge. Their eyes locked and fear sprang briefly into Nikolai's eyes. Gently he touched Don's arm. 'We have to hurry!'

The two youths noticed the fear, it was almost unmissable. They could sense that something was up but they just sat and observed. In Russia, one didn't say much. The old fears were buried deep. Memories of lost colleagues and friends still haunted the streets. They just turned their faces to the wall. The less they knew, the better.

Nikolai and Don walked hurriedly across the bridge. They were both anxious now to reach their destination, and the Embassy was a warm, welcome sight.

'Come on.' Nikolai led them off the bridge and onto the road. 'We can't go in at the main entrance. That would be too risky.' They made their way towards the small park at the back of the Embassy. Filtering in among the few trees that remained after the hurricane that had ripped through Moscow a few months earlier, Nikolai made straight for a manhole a few feet from the fountain. The fountain was still now and the water lay frozen. The moonlight was softly reflected in the icy cover, and beneath it the fish lay quiet, frozen to death. A lost sweetpaper blew across the frozen surface and landed softly on the ground, its pink glitzy exterior violating the colourless, grey environment.

Both Don and Nikolai surveyed their surroundings. They could see no one and they quickly bent down to remove the fast gathering snow from the manhole cover. Lifting it, they felt around for the rusty iron rungs that would line the side of the hole, and once they located them began to make their way down them. Don went first and Nikolai replaced the cover behind them. It would soon be covered by snow again, hiding their entrance. Nikolai followed the thin trail of light that Don made with his torch. Brushing cobwebs away and ignoring the scattering of rats around them, they made their way silently to the entrance in the Embassy. They couldn't get lost as there were no off-shoots to the tunnel.

It did not take them long to reach the manhole in the grounds of the Embassy. Slowly Don felt around for the hinge that would release the cover. Finding it, he pushed hard and the cover moved just enough for him to grasp it with his hand and push it aside. Snow fell back onto his face and he hurriedly brushed it off.

Clambering out of the hole, he found that they had emerged next to the tennis courts, well within the perimeter of the British Embassy. They could not be seen from outside now, as the high walls protected them. Nikolai lumbered out ungainly behind him and let out a silent pent up breath of air, then gulped at the fresh air, shivering involuntarily.

They stood there for a moment, quickly surveying their surroundings. They could not risk walking around to the front of the Embassy as this was the only area that had a gate, and they could be seen from the road, should anyone be looking. So instead they chose a side door in the part of the building clearly marked 'Visa Section'. They tried the door, and as luck would have it, it opened. Obviously no one had thought to lock it as it was in the secure area of the Embassy. Don made a mental note that after this was all over, he would make strong recommendations to London to beef up the security.

He had also chosen not to comment on the fact that Nikolai knew about the tunnel entrance into the Embassy, but it would be one of his first priorities to alert the security department in London once all this was over.

Entering the building they made their way cautiously up the dark, creaking stairs and found a vacant office. Don reached across the desk for the phone. Running a dirty finger down the list underneath the phone, he stopped at one name. The moonlight lit the buttons for him as he pressed the number of the one man he knew would still be there. He knew that there was a security officer on duty twenty-four hours a day, and he just hoped he would not notice the board flashing with his midnight call.

And as luck would have it, at that exact moment Barry, the security officer, put down his half eaten Marmite sandwich and glanced idly at the switchboard, and started suddenly. Leaning closer, he saw the familiar red buttons light up as a call was put through. Funny, it appeared as if this call was coming from the visa section. He knew that there was no one still in the building and he frowned, slightly agitated, drumming his fat furry fingers on the table in front of him, trying to decide what to do.

Barry sat and watched the board for a few minutes and as he watched both lights on the switchboard went out. The sandwich felt like sawdust in his suddenly dry mouth and he swallowed it in one cold, hard lump.

The Ambassador lived on the second floor of the main Embassy building, and Barry jumped slightly when his eye caught movement coming down the stairs. It was the Ambassador, and he eyed him with suspicion.

He was dressed casually in an open-necked pastel lemon

shirt and brown pleated pants. On his feet were a pair of boots and his dark fur coat was slung over his right arm. He had dispensed with his hat, so he was obviously not going far and not going to be too long. Barry was undecided as he watched him walk towards the front door. He was almost a hundred per cent sure that this outing had to do with the rather unusual phone call that he had been witness to.

The Ambassador nodded his old grey head and smiled at Barry's pale blotchy face behind the small glass partition. 'Would you mind unlocking the doors, Barry?' And almost as an afterthought he added, 'I think I'll just take the dog for a walk around the compound.' Barry knew he was making excuses, but he had no choice other than to do as he was asked. The Ambassador left with his German shepherd at his heels. The dog had been sleeping soundly and snugly in his basket near the front door, but as soon as he had heard the footsteps of the Ambassador, whom he worshipped with all his doggy heart, he was instantly at his heels.

Once outside the front door, the Ambassador made a sharp left turn and walked hastily towards the visa section. He was no longer someone casually going for a stroll, and he walked with a sense of purpose. And that purpose was Don Brett. He had known him for many years now, unofficially, of course, and admired him a great deal. He had yet to meet someone who did not like Don. His mind wandered briefly back to the first time they had met. It had been over a rather nasty little episode in Egypt that had had to be covered up. Yip, he nodded to himself, Don was definitely the goods.

He knew that Don would not be here if there was no cause for him to be. And what stood out glaringly was that if he had not been in what he considered to be great danger, he would have used the front entrance.

* * *

Barry watched as the Ambassador waved and left through the front door. He ran his hand through his short blond hair and frowned. His rugged features told of a life spent outdoors, and although he was only forty, the sun had added on an additional twenty years. He was an ugly, horrible man both inside and out.

He walked over to the reception desk, which was opposite his, and reached for his mobile phone, which he had left there earlier. It didn't take him long to get hold of the person he was looking for.

'Package has just made contact.' And he added as an afterthought, almost as if to cover himself should he be slightly wrong, although he doubted it, 'I think.'

'What do you mean, "you think"? I need to be sure, you idiot! Do you understand that?' Malcolm Pool's voice was icy on the other side. Was this guy a moron?

'I'll get back to you,' Barry said, and almost added through the phone, 'You arsehole!' He threw the phone a bit too hard down on the desk. Damn! One would figure that he had paid enough for his slight indiscretion with some prostitutes in his last post. Maybe he should just own up and make it public – but he wasn't really brave enough for that. He was rather like a sewer rat: hiding from his indiscretions, but given half a chance he would perform them again in a flash.

'I beg your pardon.' The soft voice of the Ambassador's wife reached his ears and he started.

Looking into her soft, pale blue eyes he tried to gain control of himself. 'I'm sorry, Lady Kim, that was the bank and you know how frustrating they can be.' Lady Kim knew he was lying, but her facial expressions didn't betray her. He, in turn, smiled a smile that only added to his ugliness. The bank? What was he thinking of? Of course they'd be closed at this time! And she would know it. He would have to deal with her later, he decided.

'Sure. Tell me, have you seen Rowland?' Her voice was

pleasantness itself, but Barry wasn't sure. Her short strawberry-blonde hair fell neatly into a bob around her pale face. Her lips carried just a touch of pink lipstick, but apart from that her face was bare of make-up. She was a very elegant, tall woman, slightly taller than her husband. A woman other women envied for her classic beauty. A woman with poise and dignity.

'The Ambassador took the dog for a walk.' He cast his eyes downwards and busied himself with the papers on the desk in front of him, anxious for her to be gone so he could find out more.

'Thank you.'

He watched as she put on her fur coat and disappeared through the front door after her husband.

He could hear her voice even before he saw her. 'Rowland, are you in here?' she called to him from the bottom of the stairs.

He called down to her, 'Yes dear, I'm here.'

She walked the rest of the way up the stairs and into the office where his voice was coming from. 'You were right, honey, he was on the phone.' And turning, she held out her arms to Don, whom she kissed affectionately on both cheeks. 'Hello, Don dear. In a spot of bother I hear?'

21

There was a frantic scratching on the door to John's apartment. He put his finger to his lips, indicating silence. He did not want anyone knowing about Stuart's presence here at the moment as it was safer for both of them that way. Stuart had followed John's advice to leave a brief message for his band members, saying quite simply that he had decided to go away for a few days and would catch up with them again back in the UK. At the same time, they had checked him out of his room and brought his luggage back to the apartment.

Walking stealthily towards the front door, John opened it carefully. Standing there facing him was a young woman. She was of medium height with an array of auburn hair surrounding her heart-shaped face. He was amazed at the clearness to her beautiful green eyes and cleared his throat almost involuntarily. She was standing with her head to one side and her shoulders hunched a bit because of the cold. Her eyes darted back and forth in a frantic gesture of uncertainty and nerves.

When she spoke it was barely above a whisper. 'Are you John Masters?' Her eyes were pleading – almost begging. He could sense her fear and despair.

'Yes.' He almost felt as if his voice would knock her over. He stepped out of the apartment and quietly closed the door behind him. He seemed to tower over her, which made her appear more fragile than she probably was. He didn't want to let her in the apartment, but it didn't look as if she wanted to come in anyway. She was indicating with her hand for him to follow her.

He realised that if he did so, he could be led into a trap, but he was curious and didn't sense any danger from this young woman. And he knew from experience that if something felt wrong, then it was wrong. But in this case, it didn't feel wrong at all.

'All right, I'll come with you.' Opening the flat door once more, he reached inside and grabbed his coat and hat and followed her out of the building.

Once outside, she put her hand gently on his arm and looked up into his eyes. There were tears of relief pouring down her cheeks. 'Please.' She indicated a fallen tree trunk which was secluded. The street light had not worked for ages, so they could sit there quietly, in the darkness of the night. 'Please, let's sit down then we can talk without fear of being overheard.' John reached into his coat pocket, pulled out a neat white hanky and handed it to her. She blew her nose gently, thanking him.

After a slight hesitation, she began to talk. 'I – I knew Patrick.' She paused, glossing over the fact that they had been lovers and how desperately she had loved him. She saw that she now had John's undivided attention.

'Please don't stop.' He was pressing her for more information, quite startled by her revelation. Did she really know him? Was she perhaps after something?

She continued in a quiet, agitated voice. 'I knew Patrick. I – I was helping him and, and…' She summoned up all her self-control to try and forget the horrible stench of burnt flesh that had erupted after the explosion. Some of the flesh being hers. 'I was with him when he was killed.' There, she had managed to get the sentence out.

John looked at her and exclaimed a tad too loudly, 'What?

You were with him?' This was so unexpected that he sat there, completely shocked.

'Yes. When the bomb went off, I was thrown aside into the snow. I lay there for a while but then don't remember anything else until I woke up in a flat.' She paused, taking a shaky breath. 'I couldn't move for the first few days and there was a nurse that kept coming in to see to me. But I had been locked in, kept a prisoner.'

'But why? Why would *you* be kept a prisoner?' John asked incredulously.

'I don't know. I really don't know.' She clasped her hands tightly in her lap.

He looked at her, and she returned his gaze unwaveringly, knowing that she had been right to trust her instincts. She had come to find him because Patrick had spoken of him once or twice and she had remembered it. And she was very thankful now that she had. For all his faults, Patrick had looked after her. He had rescued her from the orphanage, and now it seemed as if he was helping her from the grave, guiding her in the right direction.

He took her hand to calm her agitation. 'Please continue.' He spoke clearly and calmly and it seemed to have the desired effect on her.

Taking a deep breath, she told him, 'I know where Robert Brown is being kept.'

He battled to keep the shock from his face, but failed. 'I beg your pardon? What did you say? How do you know about that? *How could you possibly know about that?*' His mind raced and raced around his brain, collecting ideas and discarding them as quickly.

She looked up into his startled face, suddenly feeling free and full of life. She laughed softly to herself. It was finally over and she felt no more fear and she knew that she would be OK.

'But – but how?' He was confused now.

'I know because as I was creeping down the stairs to get out, I had to hide for a while in a corner on the stairs. It was dark, but below me was a room that was lit up and inside I could hear one man talking to another. They were laughing and talking together and I listened very carefully to what they were saying.' She shrugged her shoulders slightly. 'I thought that somehow you might be interested in it. I also figured,' she paused shyly, 'that maybe if I could help you, you would be able to help me with a visa and then I could perhaps leave all this behind me.'

John nodded to himself. 'If you can help us find Robert, then I'm sure that we could find some way to help you. Where is he being kept?'

'I will have to show you on the map.'

He came to a sudden decision. 'Come inside. There's someone I would like you to meet.'

She shook her head. 'No, I don't want to meet anyone.' Her eyes darted around as if expecting to be shot at any moment and a sliver of fear coursed through her.

John took hold of her hand. 'Yes,' he insisted, 'you must come with me, as you'll be safer. We need to finish our talk and it is now too cold to stay outside any longer. Come on.' He stood up and held out his hand for her.

After a brief hesitation she shrugged her shoulders and gave him her small, cold hand. He helped her up and they made their way indoors.

Once inside John's apartment, they took off their coats and shoes and John guided her down the passage, which was now dark, and into the living room. Stuart had fallen asleep, his half-empty drink sitting quietly on the table in front of him.

Natasha cast an enquiring look at John, who smiled and nodded as if to reassure her. 'He's completely harmless, so please take a seat. Can I get you anything to drink?'

She nodded, enjoying the warmth in the flat. 'Vodka please.'

As he left the room, the phone rang and John walked over to pick it up. Natasha heard his surprise, then she heard him agreeing to something. A short while later he walked in with a vodka in his hand.

'I have to go out for a minute but I won't be long. I have a key, so there's no need for you to open the door to anyone.' He handed her the drink with a steady hand.

She inclined her head towards the sleeping Stuart.

'No need to worry about him.' And as if to reassure her, 'A friend.'

She nodded, content, and he left.

Stuart stirred when he heard the slamming of a door and opening one bleary eye started slightly when he saw Natasha sitting there.

'Oh! So you're my new bodyguard.' He yawned and stretched, then looked over at her sullenly.

She just sat there quietly looking at him.

'Do-you-speak-English?' Stuart asked eventually. He overpronounced each word and spoke much too loudly.

'I am not deaf. I just choose not to speak to you,' Natasha threw back at him. What a rude man! She had been frightened, so desperately frightened for so long that all she could feel at the moment was immense tiredness. She didn't feel as if she could cope with much more.

'Oh, so you're not English?' he spoke softly.

'No.' She hoped that that would be the end of the discussion. Sitting down in a chair that was cast half in shadow, she tossed her vodka back. As it began to weave through her veins she started to feel a little better. She leant her head back and closed her eyes for a moment, wishing this man would just go away and leave her in peace.

Stuart watched as her chest rose and fell, noticing the dark circles around her eyes and the strain marks around her mouth. The white blouse that she was wearing revealed her white lace bra and a skinny frame which told of a time spent hungry. He could not, of course, see some of the bandages that remained after her harrowing experience with the car bomb.

For the first time in ages, he felt a stirring that he had thought would never happen again. She had emptied her drink and he got up. 'Would you like another?' He indicated towards her empty glass, ignoring her tired face and closed eyes, wanting her to look at him, but more importantly wanting her to notice him.

She licked the remains of the vodka from her lips, and opening her tired eyes looked directly up at him. He was startled by her direct gaze, feeling as if he was intruding on her somehow by having such thoughts about her. She handed him her empty glass, breaking the rather strained silence between them. 'Yes, please. I would love another drink.'

He sauntered out and she could hear him scrabbling away in the kitchen. He obviously didn't know where John kept his liquor. Whether that was a good sign or not, she didn't actually care.

She stood up and looked around her. Against one corner was John's bookcase and along one wall was obviously the window, with the curtains now firmly closed. She raised her hands above her head and stretched. Aah! That felt good. Slowly she lowered her arms and turned at a sound from Stuart behind her. He held out her drink. 'Vodka.'

'Thank you.' She held the glass in her bony hands for a moment before tossing it back, coughing slightly as it scratched the back of her throat. This man was doing something to her composure. She didn't quite know what it was, but she knew that she was very aware of him.

* * *

John rolled into his flat at about five the following morning. Absolutely exhausted, he just threw himself on his bed and fell fast asleep. It had been a hard night and he was pleased that it was over.

He awoke at about ten to the smell of fried eggs and burnt toast and dragged himself back to consciousness. There was a lot that they had to do today, and for a moment his mind drifted back to sleep. Struggling to pull himself back to reality, he got up and went to take a cold shower.

Emerging with the towel wrapped firmly around his waist he bumped into Natasha, who smiled broadly up at him. 'We have made breakfast for you.' She looked refreshed and had obviously showered as her hair shone. As she hadn't had any clothes with her when she had arrived, she had borrowed some from Stuart, or at least that is what it looked like.

He was quick enough to pick up on her good mood and smiled inwardly to himself. 'Thanks, I'll be with you in two secs.' Diving into his very manly styled bedroom, he tossed the huge white towel that covered him onto the thick-pile blue carpet that covered the entire floor throughout his flat, and threw on some clothes. His bed was unmade but he didn't care as he never bothered making it anyway. He figured that he was just going to mess it up in a few hours, so what was the point. The room was a sunny one, and as he pulled back the heavy beige curtains, sunlight flooded in. He liked this room. Against one wall, he had a collection of finely selected Russian country scenes, chosen for him by his last girlfriend. The relationship had not lasted very long, but her innovations in his tiny flat had survived and flourished.

It did not take him long to emerge fully clothed, and he made his way into the living room, where he found Stuart and Natasha chatting earnestly over one of his latest songs. He listened quietly for a while as he heard her softly humming it to herself.

'Yes, you need to add more words to it.' She slowly sang a

few lines to him in the way that she thought they should be sung.

'I see what you mean.' Stuart picked up on her rhythm and then stopped suddenly when he became aware of John's presence.

'No, don't get up.' John picked up his breakfast and sat down in a well-worn chair by the window. He was particularly fond of this chair as it caught the sun in winter and was a wonderful place to cosy up in over the weekends while indulging in a book.

Looking at the two heads bent so closely together on the floor, he suddenly felt a pang of guilt. They both looked so young and innocent sitting there. One could hardly believe how much trauma and angst the two of them had gone through in their young lives. Somehow it just didn't seem fair.

There was a knock on the door and both Stuart and Natasha looked up at him with questioning eyes. John nodded to them that it was OK and putting his empty breakfast plate down on the table, went to answer the door. He returned after a few minutes with two backpacks in his hands. He handed one to each of them.

'What are these for?' Stuart asked, intrigued.

John looked at him and indicated he should not ask any more questions. One never knew how many people were listening in, or what people had planted the bugs that now lay embedded in the brick. 'Thought you lot would like a change of clothes.'

Both of them still sat there holding the bags. John motioned for them to go and change their clothes, which they dutifully did.

'Where are we going?' asked Stuart as he glanced out of the window of the Trans-Siberian train which was shrieking through the silent night.

Ignoring Stuart's question completely, John proceeded along his own line of thought. 'I'm sorry I had to bring you along, but I need your help,' he said. Feeling weary after his late night, he rubbed his eyes with his hands. It had been a stressful twenty-four hours. Don had managed to get hold of him and John had told him what had happened to Robert, then together they had decided what would be the best course of action. Don had already been briefed by the Ambassador about Elizabeth but John was able to fill him in a bit more.

Don and John, together with Nikolai and the Ambassador, began organising things from their side – and asking discreet questions in order not to make too many waves and thereby jeopardise the chance of getting Robert out alive. But it was imperative that they found out what they could in the time that they had, which wasn't very much.

'I would feel better about your apology if I knew where we were going,' Stuart hinted once more, biting into an apple.

John looked at him and seemed to finally focus on the question that had actually been asked. 'We are going to Siberia.' Yawning, he stretched out on the narrow bunk opposite to where Stuart sat. Natasha had wrapped herself up in one of the grey blankets that had been provided and fallen asleep in the far corner.

Stuart continued munching contentedly mumbling, 'I don't know anything about Siberia!' And as an afterthought, 'You must be stark raving mad!'

'No, I know you don't, but you were in the army at one time and I might need your expertise. And besides' he coughed slightly, 'you are already quite deeply involved.'

Stuart turned to the sleeping form of Natasha. 'What do you need her for?'

'She can help us find a missing agent – a very important agent.'

'Natasha? What do you mean? How is she mixed up in this?' Stuart asked in surprise. He finished his apple, much to the relief of John, who found his munching irritating, and reaching over Natasha's sleeping form tugged the window open slightly to toss the core out. She shifted her position slightly but carried on sleeping.

John looked out of the grime-smudged window of the train at the icy landscape beyond. He took a deep breath and decided it was time to tell Stuart just a bit more of what he knew. After all, if he needed him, he deserved some information. Sneezing, he reached for a tissue from the box provided on the small table between the two narrow bunk beds, and hoped fervently that he was not getting a cold. The virus that he had picked up earlier in the month had left his immune system quite weak.

'I think I should tell you a bit more of what has happened here.' He watched as Stuart nodded slightly. Taking a deep breath he continued, 'Natasha was near death once. Half frozen and starved. She had been working on something with an agent – there is no need for you to know his name,' he added quickly as he saw the question rise to Stuart's lips. 'As luck would have it, he wasn't perhaps the best agent and her identity was discovered and she feared for her life. She waited in vain for this agent to arrive at their agreed rendezvous, but unfortunately, due to circumstances beyond his control, he had been detained at Heathrow.' He paused and reached towards a rather lean-looking bottle of water which also stood on the small table. Twisting the top off, he took a deep swig.

'You see,' he continued, 'she had been working at the Sodnammoc Embassy as a receptionist and quite by chance had discovered their involvement in the uprising and subsequent murder of thousands of people in Donnas. Including Anne Greeves,' he finished quietly, pausing to let his words sink in.

Stuart stared straight ahead, shocked. 'What? What did you say?'

John watched as the colour drained and returned to Stuart's face. 'I'm sorry Stuart, but the murder of Anne Greeves had a lot to do with governments being greedy for mineral wealth and having no thought of the carnage that would follow.'

Stuart glanced down at Natasha and felt an overwhelming urge to protect her. He vowed quietly to himself that he would try and keep her safe as long as she was with him and as long as he was able to. He would not let another woman he knew, and whom he had come to like, die on his watch. It would not happen again.

'Unfortunately, one or two other people that were involved are now heads of state and eager to protect their past at any cost.'

'But where is the agent that left Natasha to die?' Stuart was horrified by this.

'Dead. He died, we believe, because of his direct involvement in the death of Anne Greeves.'

'But what do you mean?' Stuart sounded a little baffled. He was beginning to feel emotionally raw at the mention of Anne. If anyone started a vendetta to avenge the death of Anne, it ought to be him. Maybe John still felt that he had something to do with it and that was the actual reason he was keeping a close eye on him? Either way, he had to see this thing through, to reach finality.

'You were not the only one who loved Anne. Her father loved her,' John said, putting down the now empty bottle of water.

Stuart froze. 'Oh my God! You're right! I had forgotten about him. Actually I thought he had died years ago. We –we – lost contact after Anne died. We tried, but in the end every time we got together it was just too painful for both of us. Too many memories. And at the time neither of us could deal with the other's grief. It was all I could do to remain sane myself.'

John nodded his head. 'I can fully understand that, but no, he isn't dead. Natasha knows where he is, because she knows him. She thinks that they've taken Robert because they believe that he was involved in the death of Anne. And I use the word "they", instead of just "him", because I believe that it would be impossible for him to do all this alone now,' he paused slightly. 'In the beginning – yes – it would have been easy, but here we have a man who does not take chances and as he found out more he would have needed more resources. However,' he paused for emphasis – 'we have to get him out of there before they kill him, and I'm not just talking about Anne's father in this case. I'm talking about some very top officials in the British government, not to mention the Russian element. They want to find and silence Robert before he reveals what he has found out about their involvement in the massacre in Donnas. Because they fear that once someone else knows, then there will be no going back.' He sighed. 'So we have to find him, and get him out safely, before he is found by the others.'

'How on earth could Natasha know Anne's father? It all seems rather bizarre.' Stuart looked across at John. 'And how do you know that he's in Siberia?'

'I know because that is what Natasha overheard, and that is all we have to go on at the moment.' John looked thoughtful. 'Whether it was intentional or not, I don't know, but we're prepared to take the chance.'

'Overheard? How? When?' Stuart was totally confused.

'That you will have to ask her.' John got up and walked out towards the toilet. It was going to be a long trip and he had no intention of divulging more than he had to. Stuart already knew a bit too much.

The train continued to ramble through the night and Stuart got up to stretch and have a walk in the run-down corridor. Both John and Natasha were fast asleep in their bunks, which he was thankful for as he needed space to put all of this into some sort of perspective in his own mind. He leant his head against the wall of the carriage and stood quietly looking out of the window at the dark night. It was bitterly cold in the corridor and he wrapped his coat a bit more tightly around him, his thoughts a million miles away.

22

A dirty snow-stained Trans-Siberian train pulled into the main station at Ekaterinburg early on the following morning. It was still dark and the lights that shone in the station were not overly bright. The trio piled themselves out onto the platform, together with a handful of other nondescript weary passengers.

Stuart looked at John. 'Where to now?' The station looked dismal to say the least.

'I think we could all do with a clean bath and something to eat.' He looked pale and felt tired. He knew that the others must feel the same. The enormity of the situation was playing heavily on his mind, which seemed to be occupied with a majority of 'if onlys' – if only they could get Robert out of there safely; if only they could know for certain that they would be safe. He shook his head dismally.

It didn't take them long to find suitable transport and ten minutes later a slightly dented taxi dropped them off at a small hotel on the outskirts of Ekaterinburg. John paid the driver as Stuart helped Natasha out.

Stuart was vaguely aware of the beginning of a new dawn and wondered idly what it would bring. Peace? He very much doubted it. Quietly he and Natasha walked towards the hotel arm in arm. It seemed odd to him that he could feel so much for someone whom he had known for less than three days. But he did feel it. He felt it very much.

John noticed their closeness and frowned slightly in the early morning light. Carrying their own backpacks, they entered the hotel. John walked straight towards the reception counter and asked the elderly Russian woman across from him, 'Do you have a reservation for Mr Smith?' Various formalities were completed and they were soon heading off to their rather dire room on the second floor. The hotel was in desperate need of some modernisation, and paint peeled heavily off the grey walls. Natasha shivered slightly and Stuart put an arm comfortingly around her.

'It's going to be OK, you know,' he whispered softly in her ear, out of earshot of John. She nodded, gaining comfort from his closeness.

It didn't take them long to reach door No. 54 and John inserted the rather rusty key into the equally rusty-looking lock and unlocked the door with a firm click. The room that greeted them was surprising: the bright yellow walls were not peeling and there was a fresh smell of cleanliness about it, after the damp smell of the corridor. It was small, but adequate, with two double beds and two small chairs near the window, facing each other across a small, round, heavily stained table. And it was light as the heavy cream curtains had been left open.

The others followed John into the room, barely noticing the faded green carpet that they trod on. They were just thankful for a clean place to hang out for a bit.

Natasha threw her rucksack down on the first bed and sat down, looking up at the two men. She watched them quietly as they put their bags down and moved to the chairs by the window. 'If no one needs the bathroom, would you mind if I went to take a bath?' They seemed almost too engrossed to notice and she moved quietly into the small bathroom taking her backpack with her.

Running her fingers quietly through the warm water, she barely noticed the heavily stained but clean bath. Idly she removed her dirty clothes and sank down into the warm, inviting water. Sighing, she closed her eyes and tried to think quietly to herself. The image of a man tortured by the death of his only daughter sprang to mind; the image of a man who had saved her, according to her nurse, and who had tenderly taken care of her wounds. Both one and the same man. It was only later that she had accidentally found out that he had been the one to cause those very same injuries, and she had confronted him angrily when he had come to see her one day.

They had sat together for ages as the dark descended around them and he had tried to explain. Tried to put into words the absolute gut-wrenching pain that he had felt when his daughter died and how he was going to make those who were responsible pay.

'But Patrick? *Why Patrick?*' she had cried out at him in anguish. She could still feel his hands on hers, holding them down with force, trying to make her understand. Willing her to understand.

'He knew what was going to happen and he did nothing – *nothing* – to warn her.' The man was consumed with bitterness and hate. 'But I took care of you. I saw you lying there in a pool of blood and I thought back to my daughter, and I just could not leave you. I had to save you.' The man reasoned more to himself than to her, as if that made things OK.

She had begun to laugh hysterically in the darkened room. 'I thought – I thought…' She could barely get the words out as her laughter turned to agonising sobs. He had held her, stone-faced, as she cried. She remembered waking up later that night to his voice talking to some stranger, and it was then that she had overheard about Robert and knew what they had done to him. Turning over, she had gone back to sleep, only to wake in the morning to find him gone. And it was that night that she had escaped. She realised that the story she told John hadn't been one hundred per cent accurate.

The bath water had gone cold and she looked down at her shrivelled fingers. Shaking away the demons in her head, she got out of the bath, drying herself with a large clean towel which had been left on the side.

On watching Natasha disappear into the bathroom, John and Stuart got down to serious business. John pulled a map out from his rucksack and laid it out on the bed for Stuart to see. He pointed to a spot a short distance away from Ekaterinburg. 'This is where Natasha thinks they have taken him.'

Stuart glanced curiously at the map. 'Why there?'

John sneezed a couple of times and reached for his hanky, 'Drat! Bloody allergies!' Blowing his nose furiously, he put the dirty hanky back into his pocket and cleared his throat before he continued. 'It would make sense as this is where there used to be an old army barracks of some kind, and it tallies with what Natasha overheard.'

Leaning closer to the map, Stuart was trying to make something of the various lines and graphs that lined it. 'This could be very interesting, but what if we are wrong?'

'There is always a possibility of that, of course, but I don't think that we are.'

They sat, quietly debating possibilities, and finally, as Natasha opened the door to the bathroom, they decided to order some breakfast. It was going to be a long day – longer than any of them had thought possible.

23

Don and Nikolai sat quietly in the train, surveying each other. They were on the same train as John had taken, but were in a different section. And they were heavily disguised. Don now sported a short, blond wig and Nikolai had shaved off his moustache and wore a heavy Russian hat pulled low over his face. It was imperative that they were not followed at this stage. They both knew that there would be no happy ending for any of them if they were captured, and they had taken every precaution that they could to prevent it.

Both men sat contemplatively, each with a blanket wrapped around his shoulders to help beat off the icy draft that wafted through the train at various times. Then, with nothing else to do, they both nodded off. The night dragged on as the train hurtled towards its destination across icy plains and past frostbitten trees.

Don stirred briefly once when there was some shouting on the train, and got up to make sure that the lock was still secure on the door. Happy that it was, he curled back up in his bunk and slept through peacefully enough. Or rather, as peacefully as one can on a Russian train which is travelling the Trans-Siberian railway.

On arrival at Ekaterinburg, they waited a while before they left the train. Dawn was just beginning to break as they left their compartment and made their way down the creaky corridor and out onto the platform. By now John should have left the station and made it safely to the hotel.

Making their way cautiously to a waiting taxi, they gave the driver the name of the hotel that John had entered an hour earlier. It did not take them long to reach it. The same woman that had greeted John at reception greeted this new party.

'Do you have a reservation for a Mr Black?' Don asked in Russian.

Nikolai's eyebrows rose, almost to the top of his head. 'Mr Black?' he whispered harshly into Don's ears. 'Could we not have thought of a more original name?'

Don smiled quietly to himself.

Getting their key, Don turned back to the receptionist. 'Has a Mr Smith checked in yet?'

Nikolai turned to Don with anguish on his face, muttering quietly to himself, 'Mr Smith? Heaven help us!'

'Yes, sir, he checked in about an hour ago. Room fifty-four if you would like to call him.' Don smiled a thank-you and indicated to Nikolai to follow him.

They made their way to their own small room on the first floor, and dismissively threw their stuff down on the neat beds before making their way direct to room fifty-four.

There was a light knock on the door and John went across to open it. 'Come in, we've been expecting you.'

Two tired-looking men walked in and plonked themselves down on the two chairs by the window. Introductions were made by John, who knew them all.

'Coffee?' Natasha offered.

'Yeah, great.' Don felt incredibly thirsty.

They sat around each surveying each other. After his cup of coffee, Don seemed to gain his second breath. 'OK, let's get to work. We don't have much time.'

'I agree with you, my friend. Time is of the essence.' Nikolai got up and sauntered off to the toilet. Don just shook his head in some amusement. He had grown to like and respect Nikolai during their time together.

John looked across at Don. 'We need to get hold of Robert quickly. The Prime Minister is announcing his plans for re-election in the next few days and we have to find Robert before that happens. I know it's tricky as there seem to be two different elements involved: a vengeful father and a sordid government.'

Don nodded his agreement. Stuart looked from John to Don. 'Do you think they know where we are?'

John shook his head. 'No, they don't know where we are at this moment, but it is likely that they will soon pick up on our trail. It means we're likely to walk directly into a trap.'

Nikolai rejoined the group and pulled out a map from his pocket. With a dirty finger he indicated to Ekaterinburg. 'This is where we are right now.' The others nodded. 'Now this,' he indicated slightly north of Ekatrinburg, 'is where the Russian government had a few "camps".'

'Yeah, John showed me earlier,' Stuart told him.

Nikolai smiled at Stuart. 'You just have to know where to look. And Anne's father knows where these camps are, as he himself trained there in his youth.'

Don turned to the others. 'Let's see what we have in our backpacks to get us started. Remember, it's going to be bitterly cold and probably extremely dangerous, so those of you who wish to back out – now is your chance.' He glanced around the small room at all their faces but no one had any inclination to abandon the task at this point.

'OK. What do you have with you, Don?' John pointed at his backpack.

'I have the bare necessities to survive for a week, and so has Nikolai. I presume you have the same?'

John nodded. 'And so has Stuart.'

Stuart nodded as well. 'Yes, I might not have been in the SAS, but I know what to prepare for.'

'OK – then it's agreed,' Don continued, 'we leave tonight.' He took another sip of his coffee and looked across at Natasha. 'But you must remain here.'

'No! You can't leave me out of this,' Natasha protested, suddenly frightened at the prospect of being alone.'

'We're not leaving you out, honey,' Stuart tried to console her. Don raised a eyebrow at this endearment and looked across at John, who buried his head in the map in front of him.

In Stuart's eyes, she had been immensely brave. His mind flashed back to his very brief encounter with Elizabeth. She too had been a very brave and strong woman, but she had died, and he would hate the same thing to happen to Natasha. 'In fact, it would be too dangerous for you to come with us.'

She opened her mouth to protest further, but John cut her short. 'Stuart is right, Natasha. You must stay here. We need a back-up in case we don't return.'

Don agreed. 'Yes, it's very important that if we fail and don't come back, the correct people are notified.' He indicated a brown envelope on the table. 'In there is a list of instructions and people who need to be contacted, should we not return.' Don looked Natasha straight in the eye. 'In effect, you have the most important role of all now.'

The others nodded silently and Natasha lowered her eyes. 'All right, I'll stay,' she whispered, not entirely convinced or happy. Don handed the envelope to her and she took it rather unwillingly.

'OK.' Don turned to John. 'What we need to do today is to buy a car – a cheap car that can take us as far as we can go.'

John nodded his agreement. 'Let's get onto that now, shall we?'

John and Don spent the rest of the day looking for and

buying a car for their expedition. It actually proved easier than they had at first thought, which was a relief to them both.

In the early hours of the following morning, four nervous men clambered quietly into a white Skoda parked in the road adjoining the hotel. Their backpacks tucked safely into the boot, they headed off into the dark morning. There was little conversation amongst them as they were all preoccupied with their own thoughts and ideas on how this would finally play itself out. They were under no illusions and realised that it was possible that none of them would be coming back. But the importance of their mission was not lost on any of them. They had discussed details and plans in depth late into the previous night.

They had been travelling for more than four hours when the road suddenly began to deteriorate. Don, who was driving, did his best, but finally had to concede defeat and pulled up. The road had been cleared at some stage, but since then more snow had fallen and the Skoda was just not equipped to deal with the amount of snow which now lay before them. And as this was not a frequently travelled road, the clearing had probably only been done once this winter.

Don exchanged a look with John, who was sitting next to him, and the other nodded. They both knew that they had come as far as they could possibly could under the circumstances.

Reaching behind him Don gently shook Stuart and Nikolai awake. 'Sorry guys, but I'm afraid that, from here on, it will have to be on foot.'

Stuart opened one bleary eye and closed it briefly. The others were already getting out of the car and he figured that he had best follow them. It was cold out and Stuart shivered, eyeing the others through sleepy eyes.

There was not much conversation between them as Nikolai took the lead and they followed him in silence. The going was not easy but still they walked, on and on. The stops were few and far between.

Nikolai used his compass to avoid getting lost. Hour after long and tedious hour they followed him. The cold and ice drained them and didn't leave much time for active conversation. And finally, just when Stuart thought that he couldn't go any further, Nikolai stopped and turned to face them. 'We're near now. I suggest we go ahead to those hills .' He indicated, in the driving snow which was becoming heavier, to the foothills of a mountain range. 'And make our home there for the present and then scout out the surroundings.'

Don nodded. 'I agree. We need to have a look around the camp before we go any further, and that should take us – how long?' He looked over at Nikolai. 'About a day?'

'Yes, that should do it.' They walked the last mile in silence. 'Let's set up camp,' Nikolai suggested when they reached the hills. They all roped together to dig out the snow and ice to make a small shelter, and they hitched up their small tent. When the job was done, Stuart threw his rucksack down and collapsed fast asleep in a corner, absolutely shattered. It had been a long time since his army days and he felt the strain of the long freezing walk, together with all the stresses and pressures of the last few days.

The other three sat quietly around a small flint fire and discussed their plans. It was agreed that John and Nikolai would set out early the following morning towards the buildings that they could see in the distance, where they hoped to find Robert. The other two would remain, and in the event that John and Nikolai did not return within a specified time frame, they would return to Natasha and take the matter from there. But they all fervently hoped that things would end favourably.

24

Robert had no idea that help was so close at hand. He glanced around his small walled prison and sighed in confusion. He looked up at the small scatchings that he had made on the wall above his head to indicate how many days he thought he had been there. Slowly he counted the lines – forty-seven. Reaching up, he scratched another line. His hand was dirty and blood-stained, and underneath the nails lay a layer of dirt. He rubbed his eyes with his other hand and felt the beard that had now grown over his face. His hand came away with blood on it. The lashings he had had this morning had left their mark. And it was this morning that he had felt a change in the men. The questions had altered slightly and he felt as if they had got what they wanted out of him. If that was indeed the case, then it wouldn't be long now before they terminated him.

He had heard a lot of commotion going on outside, with trucks coming and going. His strength was beginning to fade and he couldn't go on much longer. Not in this state at any rate. He felt starved and drained. He looked up once more to the wall and made a few more lines. Laughing, he rolled over onto his stomach and winced as his bruises touched the hard surface of the concrete. Tunelessly he began to hum 'God Save the Queen' to himself, over and over again.

25

John and Nikolai set off before the other two were even awake. Stealthily they made their way towards the distant buildings, brushing the snow from their faces as they went. On and on their boots trod, scattering the fresh snow in front of them but making no sound.

Finally and as if on cue, John indicated that Nikolai should duck. They were very close now and they could not afford to be seen. Slowly they crept forward, keeping their eyes and ears open for any sound.

They had made it to one of the outer buildings when John turned a puzzled look towards Nikolai. He leant forward and whispered in this ear, 'Don't you think that this is all a bit too quiet?' The concern in John's voice was reflected in Nikolai's eyes and he nodded. Things just did not seem right. Maybe they were in the wrong place after all? A feeling of dread passed through John; if that was indeed the case, then there would be no hope for Robert, or for them. There would be no real possibility of them getting to the UK alive if they had to spend more time looking for Robert. This was there only chance, and the strain showed clearly on their faces.

They waited there quietly, slightly hidden from view, until it had begun to get light. Then they circled the buildings slowly and carefully. There was not a sign of life anywhere. Nothing. The snow had stopped falling, and the lights from the buildings still shone, but there was no sign of a single soul. John's heart began to sink with dread.

They were standing near the door of one of the more isolated buildings when they heard a sound from within. Retreating hastily around the corner, John signalled to Nikolai that he would go back and see if he could make out anything from the keyhole. Nikolai was to stand guard and alert him if he saw anyone coming.

Nikolai hid behind a nearby bin and kept a vigilant eye on their surroundings, expecting something – *anything*. But there was nothing.

John edged quietly forward and paused at the thick wooden door. Carefully he tried to look through the keyhole and jumped slightly when he heard a voice start up with 'God Save the Queen'.

Recognising Robert's voice, he smiled to himself as he gently and very carefully opened the door. And it was there that he found him, lying with his face on the stone cold floor, singing tunelessly to himself and whoever else cared to listen.

Robert noticed the door opening slightly for the first time, and watched in idle curiosity as it got wider and wider. Opening one swollen eye as wide as it would go, he stuttered weakly, 'J – J – John? Is that really you?' as John's head popped around the door.

'None other,' said a smiling John, carefully closing the door behind him. 'Let's take a better look at you then,' he muttered as he hoisted Robert up into a sitting position. 'You've taken quite a battering, haven't you?' he commented as he surveyed Robert's wounds.

'Yip – I'm afraid so,' responded Robert weakly.

Just then the door opened and Nikolai poked his head round. Spying Robert, he walked straight up to him and grabbed him by the hand, ignoring the wincing sound from Robert, and said eagerly, 'Great to see you!'

'Nikolai!' exclaimed Robert. 'Great to see you too! Really

great … Are you really here, or am I dreaming?' he wondered almost as if to himself, and seemed to doze off.

'No, we're really here, but where is everyone else?' John asked curiously. 'We figured that we would have quite a welcoming party waiting to greet us, but there doesn't seem to be a soul around.'

'Yeah,' nodded Robert, quietly opening his eyes, 'that would explain all the to-ing and fro-ing yesterday and this morning. They were obviously packing up and moving off.' He grew quieter as the realisation that they had left him there to starve suddenly dawned on him.

John added contemplatively, 'You obviously gave them what they wanted.' There was no accusation in his voice nor any tone at all, just a mere acknowledgement of the facts.

'I'm still not too sure what that is, you know,' Robert muttered dreamily.

'What we need to work out now is how we are going to get out of here.' He looked at Nikolai and then down at Robert, who sat there with a swollen eye and dried blood all over him. He looked an absolute mess. The worrying thing was that they had left him without a coat or boots and it would be impossible for him to walk all the way back to the car in his condition, let alone without any protection from the elements.

John walked back to the door, while Nikolai sat with Robert. Pulling his cell phone from his pocket, he punched in a few numbers.

'Don, is that you?' he asked when the phone was answered on the other end, 'You're never going to believe this one – yes, yes, we got him – no, he's fine, and Nikolai is also giving him the once-over while I talk to you. But, Don, he really is in no condition to walk anywhere.' He paused as he listened to Don for a while. 'Yeah, but as I was saying, you're never going to believe this. There is *no one* here.' He listened quietly to Don's exclamation on the other end. 'They've moved camp, so it's perfectly safe for both you and Stuart to come on over. We'll wait for you, then we can discuss where to go from here. Yeah – fine.' He ended the conversation and put the phone back in his pocket.

Turning back to Nikolai and Robert, he noticed that Nikolai had removed his thermal blanket from his backpack and put it around Robert, who had dozed off again. The poor man looked exhausted, and he wouldn't be surprised if this experience would leave him mentally scarred for quite a while.

He signalled to Nikolai to follow him, and together they went outside. Standing there, leaning against the wall of the building, John said, 'I'm not too sure how we're going to get him out of here. Do you have any ideas?' He turned questioningly to Nikolai.

'No, not off-hand I don't. He is in a very poor state and there is no way that he could possibly walk the distance that we have walked, and besides, he needs urgent medical attention,' he added, grim-faced.

'Yip, one can't help noticing what a poor condition he is in. What I would suggest we do while we wait for the others is to scour the camp thoroughly in the hope that something was left behind that we could use. What do you think?'

'Good idea.' Seeing that Robert was sound asleep the two of them crept quietly from the building.

Don breathed a sigh of relief when he heard that Robert had been found alive. He even slapped Stuart hard on the back, which took him by surprise. 'Excellent news! Excellent!' He was grinning from ear to ear as the two of them walked towards the arranged rendezvous. Although they had been told by John that there was no one there, they were not prepared to ignore the chance they were walking into a trap, and still proceeded with caution.

John spotted them first and motioned them with a gloved hand to come forward.

'Where's Nikolai?' asked Don, slightly curiously.

'He's trying to fix the truck that we found,' said a smiling John, and answered Don's unspoken question. 'We've been scouting around here to try and find something that we could use to help get Robert out of here.' He paused and looked directly at Don for a moment. 'He's not doing that well, I'm afraid, so we need to get him out of here as soon as possible.'

Don nodded, saddened by the news. 'Where is he?'

John indicated one of the outer buildings. 'In there. Nikolai has made him as comfortable as possible and he is sleeping now.'

Don made as if to go in the direction that John had pointed, but decided against it as Robert was sleeping.

'Anyway,' John continued, 'we've been extremely lucky and found a discarded truck just around the other side of that building.' He motioned with his head towards a wooden building further along. It was getting cold outside and he began to stamp his feet to try and keep himself warm. 'Nikolai is trying to see if we can get it going.' As he talked, they walked around the building towards the truck. It was starting to get dark again and the snow had begun to fall quite heavily around them.

As if on cue, the sweet sound of a truck jumping to life greeted them and the beaming face of Nikolai peered round the bonnet that stood open. 'That should be fine for a short trip.' He wiped his hands on a stained cloth that he had found. 'But it will not do for a very long trip and, to be honest' – he paused slightly – 'I don't know how long it will keep going, so I would suggest that we get a move on.'

Together they manoeuvred Robert carefully into the vehicle and set off on the long and hard journey back. The truck stalled several times , but each time Nikolai managed to get it started again. Absolutely exhausted, the five of them finally tumbled out at their hotel in Ekaterinburg, thanking the stars above that they had made it. Before they carried him into the hotel, Don went ahead to have a quick peek to see if the reception area was manned. If it was, they would have to think of a distraction, but Don saw a young man behind the counter with his head on his arms and loud snores vibrating off him. Don smiled to himself. As there was no one else around he quickly returned to the others. Robert was barely conscious as Don and John carried him into the hotel and put him to bed in John's room. They didn't want to put him in a room by himself in case he took critically ill. At least here they could all keep an eye on him.

26

They did not want to wake Robert, so they spoke in hushed tones about their next course of action. A doctor had been called out earlier to have at look at Robert and he had done what he could to make him comfortable. But they knew that they had to get him out of there and safely under proper medical supervision in the UK.

After quite a lot of debate it was decided that Don, Nikolai and Robert would fly back to Moscow, and then Don and Robert would head off to the UK to try and sort things from that end. If they did it quietly and quickly, then there was every chance that they would be successful.

There was no immediate hurry for Stuart or Natasha to return, so they would take the train and leave at the end of the week. Three days away.

'What I still don't understand,' said a pale-looking Robert when he finally awoke, 'is why they left like they did.' He carried on talking quietly, almost as if to himself. 'What could I possibly have given them that made them leave in such a hurry?'

John sat quietly opposite him, with the lamp highlighting only part of his face. 'I think that you gave them some information, probably indirectly, relating to what happened during the second revolution in Donnas.'

Everyone's attention focused on Robert and they waited. Stuart silently twisted his fingers. The pain was clearly apparent on his face as the ghosts of the past seemed determined to have their say.

Robert was still very weary. His thoughts were a bit confused and his ramblings were at times a bit illogical, which was only to be expected. At one time he did look up at the others and nodded. 'Yes, I think that you are right, you know. But I wasn't involved in that operation, as you know, Don.'

'Yes, I do know, and so does John, but we also know who gave those orders – and we also know who helped the IRA with a nice lump sum, and you knew that as well. And that is why it is so important that we return to the UK with you, to try and sort this mess out, before it's too late.'

There was a knock on the door and Don went to answer it. Room service brought in the dinner. There was a small bowl of gruel for Robert as his stomach would not have been able to stand much else, and sandwiches for the rest of them.

After their light dinner, they all wearily made their way to bed. Tomorrow was going to be another long day with flights to sort out.

27

Don, Nikolai, John and Robert left the following evening as arranged.

Stuart and Natasha spent a lot of time talking and getting to know each other. They had a lot of fun during their extra two days in Ekaterinburg as they suddenly felt as if their worries were now behind them.

It was while they were on the train that Natasha came to realise that she was growing extremely fond of Stuart. They were standing in the corridor early one morning, looking out of the window. Their heads were bent close together and they laughed as they shared a joke.

Stuart gazed at her as she laughed, and smiled to himself. 'I don't know what you have planned when we get back to Moscow, but why don't we do some sightseeing together?' He paused as he could see some sort of deliberation going on in her head, 'I – I haven't seen St Petersburg and I believe that it is lovely.' He hesitated as she remained staring out of the carriage window at the passing scenery.

Then turning to him, she smiled. 'OK, I will take you to St Petersburg.'

'Great.' He returned her smile. 'Would you like some coffee?'

She nodded her assent and watched as he walked off in search of the ever elusive cup of coffee, which was served near a boiler by a vacant-looking steward. Of course, it was seldom the same boiler and the steward was inevitably missing. Therefore, tracking the coffee down was in itself an exciting challenge.

Her thoughts returned briefly to the question of St Petersburg. She had to admit that she had had a moment of doubt when he broached the subject of going there together. A moment when she wondered if her happiness would be short-lived once again. And then she had realised that she had to take the good with the bad and live her life. Really live it. It was too short to mess around with, and as those thoughts raced through her, she had agreed to go with him to St Petersburg and see where life took them from there.

The train ride seemed much shorter this time. Stuart surmised that it was the company that he kept that made it feel shorter, and it was definitely far more enjoyable.

When they arrived in Moscow, Stuart and Natasha shared a taxi back to John's apartment. He had given Stuart a key before they left and told him to make himself at home.

Part of him was disappointed that their shared adventure was now over, but another part of him was beginning to open up to this woman. It was the first time in a very long time that he had felt this way about someone other than Anne. He smiled at her, sitting so quietly next to him in the taxi, and put his arm gently around her shoulders, giving her a squeeze.

Natasha looked up at him and smiled warmly, snuggling closer to him for comfort. Upon arriving back at the apartment, he inserted his key in the door and pushed it open and Natasha followed.

Over the warm coffee that she had made for them, she smiled at him. 'You do realise that I don't have many clothes and I'll have to pop out quickly to get some things.'

'You go right ahead, my dear. Do you have any money?' he asked, almost as if it was an afterthought.

'Yes – I do now.' She looked at his puzzled glance. 'I

couldn't use the bank before as they would have known where I was. But now–' she swallowed briefly – 'now that it is all over, I can draw money without a problem.' She smiled at him and sauntered off. 'I'll see you later.'

There was no need to tell him about the telegram that she had found detailing the extent of the involvement of the Sodnammoc Embassy and the British government in the events in Donnas. She had kept a copy of that telegram and given it to Patrick, and that is where the trouble had begun. She had been seen, and she had known it when she went into work that day. The looks – she shivered involuntarily – the way they had looked at her with those cold, creepy stares, and when her boss asked if she could come into his office she had taken her chance and disappeared. She recalled how she had reached the gate, only to turn around and see a small group of them come flying out of the door after her. It was then that her terror had begun with nowhere to go and nowhere to hide. She shook her head at the distant memory of how she had waited for Patrick, and the awful cold. How he had never come, even though it had been his suggestion that they meet under the bridge. She wondered, amazed, at her desperation at the time and tried to compare it to what she felt now. But she couldn't. It was like two different worlds, and she was so damn pleased that she was here now.

Stuart watched quietly as Natasha left the apartment. Picking up the empty cups of coffee, he carried them into the kitchen and washed them, putting them on the draining board. He stood looking at his hands as he dried them on the cloth, and shivered. It suddenly felt as if it had all been a bad, horrible dream, as if none of this had been real. Anne and Elizabeth, both of them too young to die. He tossed the towel down and walked back into the lounge to look out of the window, and slowly his thoughts turned to Natasha and he smiled quietly to himself. Natasha.

28

Robert had a bad flight back to London. He was still suffering the after-effects of his recent rather nasty experience. He discussed things with Don, and decided that when this was all over that he would take early retirement.

Looking into Robert's haggard face, Don asked, 'Are you sure, Robert? I mean, I know that this has been a horrendous experience for you, but there are still possibilities open to you.'

Don was sitting next to him on the plane and Robert looked at him with exhausted eyes. 'Yes, I'm sure.' He swallowed the hard lump that had suddenly risen into his throat and he looked at Don with tears toppling out of his eyes and onto his soft, scared cheeks. 'I don't think I would survive something like this again.'

Don looked at the anguish of his friend, and realised that Robert had been frightened by the very real possibility that he would not get out of there alive. And Don could not blame him. He put one comforting hand on Robert's knee as if to offer some sort of reassurance. Robert just nodded, and curling himself up in a ball under his blanket, faced the window and fell into a disturbed and disrupted sleep.

It had been decided that John would not join them on their trip back to London as he had to sort out a few things with the Ambassador. Nikolai, likewise, would not join them as he had people at the FSB to answer to. And he had to try and find out the extent of his own government's involvement in Donnas, which had helped to create this awful mess that they had all found themselves in. He was just thankful that its involvement had not been as extensive as that of the British government. By all accounts, heads would soon roll.

Don and Robert made an unassuming entrance back into London via Heathrow airport. As soon as they had landed, Don began to make phone calls, and by the time they had cleared customs they were met by a small delegation. Robert was taken directly to hospital by two of them. 'Check him out thoroughly' said Don, casting an anxious glance over at Robert, who was sitting quietly in a corner. 'Take good care of him for me,' he told his team quietly, 'and let his wife know that he is safe and sound.' He could not let her know before now as it would risk having their plans upset, but now that they were safely back in the UK it was one of the first things he wanted to do.

He watched with some pain in his eyes as Robert, now a broken man, was gently taken and guided through a separate entrance and into the waiting ambulance. Shrugging his shoulders resolutely, he made his way out of the airport with the remaining three of his delegation following closely.

Malcolm Pool was sitting quietly behind his desk when he heard a disturbance outside his office. Raising his eyes, he watched as the door was flung back and in came Don.

Wasting no time at all, Don stormed over to his desk and slammed his fist down on it. 'You bastard! You're going to pay for what you've done! You arrogant, self-opinionated arsehole!'

Malcolm remained seated, and looking up at the spitting Don tried to appear unruffled. He raised his hand to his tie and suddenly grabbed at it as if it was suffocating him. Hastily he tore if off and flung it at Don.

'You're a coward! You hypocritical pig!' the CDS spat at Don. 'You have no idea when you have it made.' He stood up and faced Don, equally furious. 'You had to go and poke your nose in and ruin everything!' He swept a glass of water off his desk. 'You don't even know what you're doing! You've ruined this government – this country – with your bullshit attitude! Now get the fuck out of my office!' he shrieked at Don, spit gathering angrily in the corners of his white clenched mouth.

'You blood-sucking leech! That's all you are,' Don threw at him as he made his way out of his office, 'and you're going to pay for your actions in blood! You had no right to support that revolution in Donnas. No right to take away those people's freedom and their lives!' Don slammed the door behind him with such force that he could hear a picture fall off the wall, but he was past caring. They were going to pay for what they had done. For what they did to a whole nation where they had no right to be, interfering for no other reason than its mineral wealth; and for what they did to Robert. It made him feel physically sick.

Ultimately, though, what they had underestimated was the love of a half-deranged grieving father. A father's love. The love Anne Greeve's father had for her, and now his absolute obsession with making everyone pay for what they had done to her. Don doubted if they would be able to stop him now, and part of him was glad.

As he left the building he was faced by a sea of journalists and he smiled to himself.

Malcolm sat down shakily after Don left and just sat staring at the wooden door in front of him. Finally he reached for the phone and dialled. 'The game's up, I'm afraid.' He replaced the receiver and got up to pour himself a stiff glass of Scotch. Back at his desk, he idly watched while the light picked up its different shades of amber. Finally he reached into his pocket and pulled out a key, which he inserted in the bottom drawer of his desk. He opened the drawer and pulled out his revolver. Gripping the glass in one hand, he downed the liquid. At the same time he raised the gun to his temple and fired one shot.

Unfortunately, the shot did not kill him. The press were to report weeks later that Malcolm Pool would remain in a vegetative state for the rest of his life. True justice.

29

John was sitting with the Ambassador in his private residence. They each held a glass of Scotch. John raised it silently to his lips and took a sip. The liquid flowed smoothly down his throat and he swallowed contentedly.

'Well!' exclaimed the Ambassador, turning his glass slowly around in his hand.

'Well, is not quite the word I would use,' said Lady Kim. She was sitting comfortably across from the two men doing some needlework, and she put it down next to her on the arm of her chair. 'Who would have thought it?' She stretched her long slim legs out to the warmth of the fire.

'Indeed,' said John, raising one dark eyebrow and taking another welcome swig from his glass.

The Ambassador leant over to reach for his pipe, which lay on the table. Putting his glass down next to him, he carefully loaded the tobacco and lit it. Taking a few puffs, he relaxed back into his chair.

'Yip, I suppose you are right there, my dear,' he said idly while blowing out smoke. Their spoilt dog, which had been lying at his feet, got up. He gave the Ambassador a filthy look as he hated smoke, and made himself comfortable at Lady Kim's feet.

'Ooh – you're heavy!' She tried to nudge him off, but gave up as the dog had assumed a dead weight and it appeared as if nothing on earth would shift him now.

'At least Barry is now in prison,' said John, feeling warm and cosy. 'He had been working for Malcolm Pool all along. Seems as if Malcolm had some hold over him, some business with prostitutes or something like that. I am sure that the exact details will become clearer to a very few in time. And of course, Barry being the snivelling creature that he is, fell into the trap like a bee to pollen. A really nasty man, and now he will be screaming his innocence and calling on all sorts of names to help him out.' He paused. 'But I guess no one will be paying too much attention to him.' They had all enjoyed a very informal dinner and were now relaxing around the fire. He loved this room, and as he looked around he admired the intricately carved woodwork around the doors and fireplace. 'Good thing you were able to detain him before he got away.'

The Ambassador stretched. 'In the end, he was too arrogant for his own good. Evil bastard. He is, of course, going to be tried for the murder of Elizabeth here in Russia as the crime was committed here. And let's be honest, to all intents and purposes it would be too embarrassing for the UK if he was tried there and things got out.' He then added as an afterthought, 'Hope he gets what he deserves.'

John nodded. He had been to the prisons in Russia, and there was no doubt that he would get what he deserved.

'There is no chance of him getting off?' Lady Kim raised her eyebrows questioningly.

'No – none,' replied her husband. 'Please pass me the paper, love.' Lady Kim passed it over to him. 'Thanks.' He put the paper down on his knees and turned to John, 'Guess you'll be leaving us now?'

'Yes,' he yawned sleepily. 'Now that almost everyone in the Embassy knows my true role here, there's no point in staying. Who knows where I will be in a few weeks.'

'I hope you will keep in contact, John,' Lady Kim picked her needlework back up.

John sat there, comfortably watching the fire and slowly drinking his drink. Don had been in touch with him earlier that day, telling him what they had found in the locked locker at Heathrow. There was enough evidence there to hang Malcolm Pool and the PM, not to mention various members of the Russian government, which would be handed over to Nikolai. When all the information had been gone into, it appeared as if Malcolm Pool and the PM had acted by themselves for their own financial gain. Deluding others about what was actually going on, they had been able to secure funds and resources to help with the uprising. It was quite remarkable how they had managed to succeed with their deceit.

Sighing peacefully, he reached for another drink.

30

The hotel where Stuart and Natasha were booked in was right next to St Isaac's Cathedral. As the sun rose it caught the beautiful golden dome in a bowl of light.

'Isn't that beautiful?' remarked Stuart to Natasha as he caught a glimpse of the dome.

'It is lovely,,' agreed Natasha. 'I've always much preferred St Petersburg to Moscow. There just seems to be more life here and more acceptance of the way things are. I sometimes find that the Moscovites are uninterested in the rest of the country. I presume that it is because they are the wealthiest part of Russia and therefore look with disdain on the rest.' She paused contemplatively, shrugging. 'But what they do not seem to realise is that the others don't think much of them either.'

She smiled up at Stuart, who wrapped his arms tightly around her. 'You know, I think that I have had enough of politics to last me a lifetime! All I need is you!' he told her.

'Maybe that is not such a bad thing after all,' she said warmly.

It didn't take them long to check into their room, and while they sorted out their luggage Stuart leant over and turned on the TV. Suddenly what was actually being said on the CNN channel dawned on them and they sat down on the bed in shock, the words seeming to flow over them:

There is still no word on the sudden and unexplained disappearance of the British Prime Minister. The riddle looks as if it is going to remain unsolved at the moment. As you can well imagine, British politics is at this moment in total disarray, with the deputy Prime Minister taking over. Word is that new elections will be held sooner than expected.

'Well!' said Stuart. 'It's really finally over, isn't it?' He turned to Natasha.

'Yes,' she said quietly, 'it's finally over.'

He reached for her and pulled her to him and kissed her tenderly on the lips. She returned his kiss with love.

He sunk back into a quiet corner at the back of the taxi and closed his eyes. Weariness overwhelmed him and he slept. He had done all he had set out to do. Of course he had valued the help of the men he had gathered together in order to fit the last puzzle piece in place, but that is all they had been to him in the end. Just men – helping to dish out his vengeance. And they had needed the money. What they were now going to do with that money he had no idea and he didn't want to know. But seeing as the majority of them had been from Chechnya he had a strong inkling. But that was not his concern.

Suddenly the taxi ground to a halt and he stirred. Reaching into his pocket he pulled out a bunch of notes, not really caring that it might be too much and the taxi driver dribbled his greed. He alighted and looked around this quiet and desolate area of Warden Bay on the Isle of Sheppey and finally began to feel peace as he looked out over the ocean in front of him. He would soon hold his daughter in his arms again. His beloved Anne.

The rain was beating down softly around him but he hardly noticed as he climbed off the wall and onto the wet sand. The tide was out so he would have to walk out to meet it. As he walked he began to discard his clothes in an effortless motion to free himself of the last trappings of sanity.

In some insane way, he felt content that he had not murdered Robert. And illogically he surmised that he had done him a favour. Robert had given him the last bit of information he needed to complete his task. He had told him about the telegrams that the Prime Minister had tossed into the bin. Telegrams that could have saved his daughter. Knowledge that he just tossed away as if it didn't matter to anyone – not a soul – not the starving or dying and in particular, not his daughter. *His daughter!* None of them understood that. Why was it so difficult for them? They had casually discarded the one thing left to him in this world that actually meant something to him and they had just thrown it away.

A stream of clothes lay stretched out on the beach behind his naked body. The fate of the Prime Minister would in time become known, but for now *he* felt free, and it felt good. Stretching his arms to the sky he screamed out in unreleased joy at succeeding, and with exciting anticipation at his death he threw himself into the bubbling sea where the currents quickly submerged his last insane ravings, burying them forever.